MW01100986

Going Home

BY

Veronica J

Order this book online at www.trafford.com
or email orders@trafford.com

Most Trafford titles are also available at major online book retailers.

Note for Librarians: A cataloguing record for this book is available from Library and Archives Canada at www.collectionscanada.ca/amicus/index-e.html

Printed in Victoria, BC, Canada.

ISBN: 978-1-4251-7479-8 (sc)

We at Trafford believe that it is the responsibility of us all, as both individuals and corporations, to make choices that are environmentally and socially sound. You, in turn, are supporting this responsible conduct each time you purchase a Trafford book, or make use of our publishing services. To find out how you are helping, please visit www.trafford.com/responsiblepublishing.html

Our mission is to efficiently provide the world's finest, most comprehensive book publishing service, enabling every author to experience success. To find out how to publish your book, your way, and have it available worldwide, visit us online at www.trafford.com

Trafford rev. 7/16/2009

www.trafford.com

North America & international
toll-free: 1 888 232 4444 (USA & Canada)
phone: 250 383 6864 • fax: 250 383 6804 • email: info@trafford.com

The United Kingdom & Europe
phone: +44 (0)1865 487 395 • local rate: 0845 230 9601
facsimile: +44 (0)1865 481 507 • email: info.uk@trafford.com

I would like to dedicate this book to a guy in a band, who proved to me that dreams really do come true.

Thank-you

Chapter One

"Hello",

She paused as she looked around the room. All these people she thought, who are they?

"Good Evening, my name is Robin Cotton." She spoke in her acquired southern accent. "Some of you may know who I am, some of you may not. I graduated with y'all twenty years ago! Tonight we are here to celebrate the twentieth anniversary of our graduation! Twenty years, where have they gone? I am thrilled to be here tonight and was touched when I was asked to be master of ceremonies for tonight's event. Some of you know, I am married to a very special guy and we live in Texas. Just between Austin and Houston. When we got the invitation to this event, my husband Lee thought it would be fun to ride from Muldoon Texas to Victoria on our Harley! And yes we did it! Does anyone know how it feels to travel thousands of miles on the back of a Harley Davidson motorcycle?" The crowd in the room laughed.

"I sure hope there will be some good dancing tonight cause I don't think I will be able to sit down for a week! It was so much fun!

We didn't exactly ride all the way, we had a few semis as escorts. If the weather got bad we loaded the bikes onto one of the trucks and met at the next stop. You will find out in a little bit why we had a few semis's following us.

We saw a lot of sights and visited many places we had never been to before, but the best sight of all was coming home to Victoria!" The room exploded in applause and whistling.

"I used to think this was such a big city, and it certainly has grown. In Lee's line of work we travel a great deal and we've been to many cities and towns, and even though we live in Texas, there is nothing and I mean nothing as beautiful as Victoria!"

The crowd started to applaud and cheer and whistle again.

"I tend to ramble on when '*I* 'get the opportunity to be in front of a microphone. Anyway, for those of you who have stayed in this city, I hope you are proud of the way it looks and how it has grown. Because now you are the people who are responsible for the way it looks, the atmosphere, the crime and violence, the peace and beauty. And just to think twenty years ago, when we left school we thought we had the world in our hands. Little did we realize at that time, we some day would. How young and naïve we were. The old expression, if I knew then what I know now, holds more truth to it than we could ever have thought possible back then.

Among us tonight we have homemakers, blue collar workers, white collar workers, business men and women, teachers, civil servants, nurses, doctors, lawyers, and oh yes maybe a chef and a musician!"

She paused again and looked for Lee in the crowd. Where was he? How could he be late for this? Maybe he wouldn't show up at all. Thoughts were running through her head. Oh how she wanted to show him off to everyone. The snotty girls who never talked to her in school and to the ones who thought they were better than everyone else. And to all the guys who she had crushes on who had never asked her out. She hated being like this, thinking this way. It wasn't like her. But she was nervous and excited to be coming back home as somewhat of a celebrity. I guess anyone in the same circumstance would feel the same way she thought to herself. Finally she spotted Lee standing alone against the far wall. As far as she was concerned, he was the most gorgeous man in the world. He was almost six feet tall, one hundred eighty seven pounds of solid muscle, the darkest blue eyes she had ever seen and his hair.... It was long and naturally curly and hung halfway down his back. A light brown color that was streaked with blonde after days spent in the sun. He was wearing black jeans, a white tuxedo shirt, black bow tie, a black Country style tuxedo jacket designed by "Manuel", the best Country wear designer in Nashville. And even though she couldn't see them, she knew he had on his black and white snakeskin Tony Lama cowboy boots. How could she not have noticed him in this crowd? He looked like a God to her. Their eyes met. He gave her his knee-weakening smile. She smiled back at him and felt a calm inside her. He was there and he looked proud of her. How could she even think he wouldn't be there? She continued with her commencement speech feeling secure and confident now.

"Some of our fellow graduates didn't make it this far, God had other work for them to do. But for those of us who have made it through the past twenty years, it's been a struggle and a challenge. In my case it's been all that and fun as well. I hope that your past twenty years have been fun and if they have been more of the struggle and challenge, then now is the time to have the fun. Now is the time to do all those things that you never have had time to do. The kids are getting older, you are starting to get your freedom back. Or maybe you are just starting to have a family, you have done all the fun stuff and now its time to settle down. Whatever your life brings, make sure you take each day as it comes and have a little fun. Laugh as much as you can. Plus, make sure to enjoy each night as best as you can. The last several years for me have been all about the nightlife. It's when our wild sides get to come out and we can relax at the end of a long hard day doing something we enjoy." The audience began to giggle. "No, I'm not talking about sex, for those of you with those smiles on your faces. You will all see in a little bit what I mean. Starting with tonight let's all pretend we're back in high school again with no cares no worries, no responsibilities. Let's have fun tonight and this weekend! And let's enjoy the next twenty years for I have a feeling, they will go by very quickly!"

Everyone applauded and looked excited to begin the festivities.

"I just have a couple more things to say. And to explain why all those semi's are parked outside. No it's not my wardrobe! I moved to Texas to study cooking and have become a chef specializing in Southwest cuisine. I met my husband while I was at the Texas Southern University. He was a struggling music student and a regular at the restaurant where I did my practicum. We sort of hit it off and have been together for the past seventeen years. Well, tonight, I'm not going to be doing any cooking but my husband is no longer a struggling music student, he is the lead singer and guitar player for the country group of the year.........Rocket Fuel!"

Suddenly the crowd went wild, cheering, clapping and whistling. Robin heard people saying, "Wow, she's married to him!"

"Thank-you!" Robin beamed.

"Not only did Lee and I ride here on Harley's, the entire band came along for the road trip. We took a group vacation. The rest of the guys will be here later to play for you. And that is what I meant by "night life". This is how we spend our nights. Travelling and performing all over the world. For people like y'all to be able to sit back, relax, and enjoy the show. We all hope you enjoy Country music and if you don't maybe we can convert you tonight. Actually if you don't enjoy country music please don't worry. The band will only play for about an hour and then we will have canned music. So thanks again." She glanced over to one of the caterers who signaled that the dinner was set up and ready to go. "I'm now being told dinner is ready so let's start with the first table to my left and then the first table to my right and take turns from there. Enjoy!"

The audience clapped loudly and Robin could see the look of anticipation in their faces as she glanced over the crowd.

Robin turned off the microphone and spoke to the reunion organizer about what would happen next and when she would need to be back on stage. She then went and found Lee. He gave her a kiss on the cheek, put his arm around her shoulders and together they went and found their table.

Chapter Two

Robin was five foot four with long thick blonde hair and pretty aquamarine blue eyes. She was in great shape. She hated working out, but with a professional husband she needed to keep herself looking good. For many reasons. The main one being that each night Lee performed he had numerous women making all sorts of tempting offers. Robin felt the only way to compete with some of these women was to look better than any of them and to make him want to come home to only her.

For years keeping up the image she had made for herself was wearing her down. She felt uncomfortable every time Lee left town. She felt she should go on each road trip with the band just so she knew what he was up to. She did trust him. It's just that with all that temptation, sometimes love and trust gets forgotten. She had seen it happen many times with the other guys and it had happened to them over the years as well.

Tonight she was wearing a black velvet cocktail dress with white silk straps that went under the arm and up around the neckline in a halter style. The dress totally accentuated her small waist and ample bustline. She had on soft black stockings and wore white satin pumps. She wore the diamond stud earrings

Lee had given her for their tenth wedding anniversary and a matching diamond necklace and bracelet he had bought for her after the band had signed their first record deal and had their first number one hit. Robin and Lee's attire complimented each other. Whenever they went out to a function like this, Robin made sure they looked like they belonged together.

They sat at a table with two of Robin's closest girlfriends from school. Most of the people in the room were total strangers to her now. She had been gone for so long. Her girlfriends Sara and Pam were the only ones she still kept in touch with. She was on the road with the band so much, that it was usually a postcard from every city they traveled to and long catch up phone calls when Robin got home. Every now and then when Robin needed a comforting talk with someone not connected to the entertainment world, she would call Pam or Sara, just to talk and get caught up with the life she'd left behind. Another life so completely different from her own and those lives sometimes, she was so very jealous of. Christmas was always a time to be in touch. With gifts sent to the kids and visits made if possible, but always somehow, someway to fit in a conversation.

Sara's husband Glenn was a dump truck driver. He had been doing this since he graduated from school, two years before they did. Sara and Glenn had two children a boy and a girl. Sara was a stay at home mom. She felt her family was more important than material things. They lived in a simple house in a residential neighborhood and had some good times and some bad times. Mostly they struggled from paycheque to paycheque. Robin was the godmother of their children, so from time to time as her and Lee's life got better, she would send great gifts for the kids birthday's and Christmas's.

Pam and her husband Marty had one child, a boy who was seven and they were expecting their second child in a month. Pam had been the wild one of the three. She was always good for a laugh. Sometimes they would laugh so hard they cried. She had played the field before settling down with Marty, but it was obvious that they were very much in love. Robin admired Pam for waiting and finding the right guy. Of the three of them, Robin felt Pam was the happiest. Life just came easy for them. She had been a stewardess for Can Air for about ten years before she met Marty. She had traveled extensively and dated any man who asked her out. Marty had been at the Victoria International Airport for about six months when he and Pam met. They had seen each other now and then at work, but when they went on their first date, they both knew they were in love. After about two months they moved in together and a month later they got married. Fast and furious, just like Pam.

As they all sat together reminiscing of old times and trying to remember who was who, Robin and Lee glanced at each other and smiled. They too were very much in love. Their road however, had been traveled a little too much on the rocky side. They now, Robin felt, had come full circle and were back in love again. They had been trying to have children for a few years with no luck. It actually hadn't been a priority until lately. Lee's career had taken top priority all these years.

Chapter Three

Robin had met Lee in Houston Texas. She had moved to Texas in 1977 a year after she graduated high school. The year after graduation was spent trying to decide what she wanted to do with her life. The guy she had dated through grade eleven and twelve had dumped her two weeks before graduation. His name was Don Land. What a shock! Looking back now she couldn't understand how she felt she was in love with him. But, he was the guy she was going to marry. With that on her mind she did not make any career plans. As far as she was concerned her future would be wife and mother. What more was there?

She had lost her virginity to Don when she was sixteen years old. They had met in the summer of 1974. She worked at the local ice cream parlor close to the lake. He didn't have a summer job. He hung out at the lake everyday and would come by every afternoon to get an ice cream. They would talk and flirt. Finally one day he asked her out. She had been on dates with other guys before, but she was really nervous and excited about this one. He was one of the coolest guys at school. Most of the girls would give anything to go out with him. And some of them had. Robin had only heard this of course, but she would go on this date with an open mind and remember all the things her Momma had taught her.

They went to a movie and then to a coffee shop for a coke and fries. He took her home on time and gave her a great goodnight kiss on the lips. He hadn't tried anything more.

When they went back to school that September, Robin hadn't realized how beautiful she had become over the summer. She had matured into a young woman. Her hair was bleached by the sun, and she had a great tan, which made her eyes look even bluer. She had grown a few inches and had developed quite the curvaceous body. She was now sixteen years old and a lot of guys noticed her. She was oblivious to the attention, as she couldn't see how she had changed. But Don noticed all the guys noticing her. He started paying a lot more attention to her. For Christmas that year, he gave her a gold necklace with a gold heart shaped charm on it. By the following spring he was ready to make his move.

Robin still hadn't realized that anyone else could possibly be interested in her, after all Don made sure he took up all her free time. He still didn't work. It was a good thing he had rich parents. They had bought him a car when he turned sixteen, paid for the insurance, the gas, and he got an allowance each week just to have fun with. His parents thought that kids should have fun and enjoy their youth. But they had to study hard and have good grades in school. Don was lucky there. He was very smart and he was also very charming and smooth. He could talk his way out of, or into, anything. Which he quite often did.

During spring break of that year, Don's family had decided to take a vacation to Disneyland. Of course they had expected Don to go with them. However he had other plans. He told his parents that he had to study to get some extra credits for a class he was taking. As usual they believed him and felt it was more important that he maintain his grades than go to Disneyland again. After all they had just been two years earlier. Don had everything planned. Robin knew his parents were away and she was actually looking forward to having some really private time with Don. They had fooled around in the car at the beach and at the lake. Only kissing, touching and feeling. To Robin, that was serious enough. She wanted to save herself for the guy she was going to marry. Don knew this and had done all the smooth talking and convinced Robin he was in love with only her and they would one day get married. During spring break Robin had to work most days. She did have the last Friday night off. Don said he would cook her dinner at his house. She arrived about six o'clock. He had prepared steak and prawns, baked potatoes, and a salad. He had managed to get into his parent's wine cellar and found a bottle he didn't think they would miss. He had candles lit, the dining room table set with his mothers best china, crystal, and silverware. Robin was impressed. The dinner was good for a guy who only knew how to cook Kraft dinner.

The wine was heady and Robin could feel she wasn't in total control. She felt good though and she knew what was going to happen that night. She was in love with Don and wanted to prove it to him. After dinner he lit the fireplace in the living room. They went and lay on the carpet in front of it. Don had filled their wineglasses again and he had put on some music. Not the kind they were used to listening to but some soft romantic kind. They started to kiss. Softly at first, then more passionately. He undid her blouse, she undid his shirt, he undid her bra and removed the blouse and the bra. He softly started kissing her breasts and caressing them. This was the first time he had seen them totally uncovered. He had felt them many times before but Robin would not let him see them. He was awestruck. They were beautiful, full and firm. Robin felt so much in love at this moment. But she wasn't really sure what to do next. She could feel him grow as he lay on top of her and kissed her. She asked him if he had any type of birth control and he nodded yes and conveniently pulled a condom out of his jean's pocket.

Before she knew it they were both naked on the floor. The fire was warming their bodies and the wine had already warmed their passion. They kissed a while longer. He put on the condom. Then the big moment came.

Robin could feel Don jabbing at her in a rushed, hurried frenzy. She wasn't sure if this felt good or was painful. Before she knew it he was rolling off of her, kissing her lips and telling her how great it was. That was it. She excused herself and went into the bathroom to get dressed. While she was pulling on her panties she found a small wet spot of blood on her thigh. She was no longer a virgin.

Over the next several months, they had sex the same way about four times. It was over and done with before Robin even knew it.

By the following spring they were fighting quite a bit. Don wasn't around as much and he was spending more time with the guys. At least that's what he told Robin.

In May, Robin found out he had been dating two other girls from school. She wasn't really surprised, but she was very hurt. This was not how it was supposed to end. After giving herself to him, with the thought that one-day they would be married, she had hoped he could have at least told her. They could have talked about it and left as friends who had shared a very important 'first' in both of their lives, but of course it came from one of his friends.

Paul had called Robin from time to time looking for Don or wanting to hang out with them. He was a nice guy and a better friend to Robin then he was to Don. And even though him and Don were friends, he was nothing like Don. They had talked about all kinds of things. Life and love, world events, but this night he had called and asked Robin to meet him at the ice cream parlor.

He was there waiting when she arrived. Robin could tell he was nervous or anxious about something. She asked him what was wrong and he started with "I don't know how to tell you this...........". She knew what was coming. She started to cry. Paul hugged her and held her tight and let her get it all out. She asked how Don could do this to her, but Paul didn't know. He felt bad for Robin and the way Don had treated her. She was a great girl and Paul said that he would never have treated her this way if she were his girlfriend. Robin started to laugh. Through her tears, she said now she didn't have a date for graduation and Don had two. Paul said he would be more than happy to take her to graduation. And he did!

Chapter Four

Robin looked around the room. She was looking for Paul and Don. She didn't really want to see Don, but she did want to see how time and two divorces had affected him. Paul and Robin would always have "something". They went to graduation together and hung out together a lot before Robin decided to move to Texas. They enjoyed each others company and had very long life talks and shared their deepest thoughts with each other. But Paul wasn't really Robin's type. He was a nice, kind guy with a heart of gold, but he couldn't make his mind up about anything. Anything Robin wanted to do, they would do. She had to decide everything. Where they would eat, what movie they would see, even what clothes he should wear. It was like having another girlfriend. They never got romantically involved either. They would hug and that was as far as it went. He was a good friend in a time of need. So it wasn't really hard when she decided to leave, at least not as far as her and Paul were concerned.

She spotted Paul. He hadn't changed much. He was a little on the thin side. He still had most of his hair and he smiled just the same as he did in school. He was sitting with his wife. Don was there too with either a wife or girlfriend Robin assumed. Paul waved at Robin and then his entire table turned and looked and waved. Robin was a little embarrassed, but she waved back. Don looked awful. She couldn't quite believe it was him. Twenty years had certainly taken their toll. He was bald on the top of his head, he had a beer belly and looked really out of shape. He glanced over at Robin and she caught him looking. She looked away. The feelings she had at that moment made up for every insecure, self-conscious moment that had happened in her life. In a split second, she felt wonderful and beautiful and loved and proud her husband looked so damn good and that he was who he was. She almost felt sorry for Don. Almost. It wasn't as though what had happened between her and Don was the worst thing that had ever happened to her in her life. It was just something that, probably because of the age she had been, and the fact that he was her first real love, had made a significant impact on her relationships with every man since.

Robin's table had finished dinner. They were having dessert and coffee. Lee was getting along fine with the other guys. They were asking all kinds of questions about his work, life on the road, girls, hotels, girls, buses, girls, Harley's, girls, all the other big country stars he had met, girls! The conversation always came back to girls. There were so many women out there who would do almost anything to be with a star and with looking as good as Robin thought Lee was, so did millions of other women. He had plenty of stories of what women did to him and the other guys in the band. Robin had heard them all before and it bothered her. Despite how she had felt a few minutes ago, she felt insecure again. How could she not be? Why did he stay with her? Would he leave her one day? Was he just staying for the convenience and a place to come home to? Maybe he had other women in other towns. 'Oh God' she thought, why am I thinking of this here and now? He came with me. So just enjoy the weekend and have fun. She turned and looked at Lee and smiled. He put his arm around her and said, "But this is the best woman in the whole world. She keeps my feet on the ground".

He then kissed her. Robin wondered if this was all a show. '*Oh stop it*!' she said to herself. And she put her hand on his thigh and kissed him back.

The reunion organizer announced that dinner was now finished and on the walls were posters with pictures of everyone from the class with information sheets that they wanted everyone to fill out. This was to get all classmates updated as to how long they had been married, where they worked, how many kids, etc. She also announced that the rest of the band had arrived and would Lee Cotton please meet them backstage. There was going to be about half an hour for everyone to mingle and then the music would start.

Robin got up to go with Lee. She wanted to walk around and stretch her legs. They went out the main doors and found the backstage entrance. Joe, Billy, Jon and Bo were getting things set up. They had gone to a Pub for a few beer and dinner before coming to do the reunion show. Robin could tell they had had a few. They looked like they were ready to party. All she hoped was that they could keep it together until they had performed for awhile. The women, Ashley, Becky, Virginia and Sue decided to find a nightclub in town. They felt this was not their party and didn't really want to hang around. Robin was grateful. After all, she herself didn't feel all that comfortable being here. Lee and the guys warmed up. When they were ready, Robin stepped on stage and with a microphone in hand asked,

"Did everyone enjoy dinner?"

There was a big round of applause.

"Thank you to the caterers for the great food." Then she added jokingly,

"I, of course, would have served a much different meal!"

Everyone laughed.

"I hope tonight that we all get a chance to mingle and to talk to people who we haven't seen for a long time. But right now I would like to introduce some of my favorite people. A bunch of guys who I love very much. I would like to add a very big heartfelt thank you on behalf of all of us here, to them for travelling all the way from Texas for our entertainment tonight."

More applause and whistles.

"So please make welcome, Rocket Fuel!"

The band started playing. Lee was standing there looking totally sexy. He had changed into a white dress shirt and a black leather vest. The hair on his chest could be seen at the top opening of the shirt. He had a gold chain around his neck that Robin had bought him for their tenth anniversary. A gold guitar and gold treble clef on it gifts from Robin for the last two albums the band had cut. And of course, the black and white Tony Llama snake skin boots. Lee had a closet full of cowboy boots at home, but these were his favorites.

The rest of the guys were dressed the same, black jeans, white shirts, black vests. They all looked very sexy too! They were singing their latest hit, which was number two this week on Billboards Country Chart. They were hoping for number one next week. That would be fourteen number one hits. These guys were hot.

Chapter Five

It was September, and the days were very warm, but the nights cooled off quickly. Robin stepped outside to get a breath of fresh air. It was hot in the auditorium. Most everyone was up and dancing. They all seemed to be enjoying the band. A few people had come and talked to Robin. The ones she remembered she asked how their lives were now and what they were up to. She saw Paul over to the side having a cigarette. '*He never used to smoke,'* she thought to herself. She walked over to him and gave him a big hug. He picked Robin up off her feet as he hugged her back. She felt a comfortable feeling for a moment right then. He pushed her away still hanging onto her hands, and took a good look at her. Then he pulled her back in and hugged her again.

"Oh Robin you look better now than you ever did in school. It's so good to see you, it's been too long!"

Robin laughed. "You look good too and thank-you and yes it has been a long time."

When she had come home for visits, she would call Paul and they would get together. But after a few years the visits became less frequent and she stopped calling. After her parents moved to

Texas seven years ago, she had not made a trip back to Victoria till now.

They stood there with their arms wrapped around each other. Paul pointed out a few of his old friends and when he put names to the faces, Robin began to remember most of them.

"How are you really doing Robin?" he asked, as he turned her towards him to look in her eyes. Her eyes, he remembered, were so beautiful. If you looked into them when she talked or even when she was just thinking you could tell just how she felt.

"Fine Paul. Just fine." She smiled.

"That's it, just fine?" He exclaimed. "You're married to one of the hottest guys in the world right now and you're just fine!?"

Robin was laughing. She hadn't remembered Paul ever getting this excited.

"Well then I'm more than just fine, I'm great!" she said in between giggles.

Paul doubted her. He wanted to know the truth. At that moment he felt like her big brother. And those eyes. They told more in a glance than the words that she spoke.

"I don't believe you Robin. You don't have that sparkle in your eyes that you used to get when you were happy."

"Oh damn you Paul! After all these years you still know how to read me. The truth is, I am doing great. My life is busy. I travel with Lee most of the time. We have a four hundred and fifteen-acre ranch in Texas, with ten horses, some cattle, some goats and chickens, three dogs and I think about five barn cats. We have some beautiful gardens and I try to putter in them when I'm at home. We own a Honkey -Tonk Bar and Grill in town. I try to keep track of that when I'm around. Lee's parents and my parents each have homes on the ranch with us. They look after things when we're on the road." Robin was uncomfortable describing the things that they had obtained in their life. She knew they had a lot and that they had a very comfortable life, but she didn't want to come across as being better than, or having more than, anyone. She knew that one day the fame and fortune would end and what they had obtained in the last few years would have to get them through the rest of their lives. It could all end with the next upcoming Country Star.

"I guess the sadness you see in these eyes is because when we come to things like this I realize what I'm missing in my life. We don't have a normal life. I never know where my husband is going to be. He's in a different city every night. We don't have any children. Paul I'm thirty-eight years old and I feel that I'm running out of time. Lee's career has taken priority the last few years. The hell the last few, its been ever since I met him. Don't get me wrong, I don't begrudge my life for a second. We've had and still do have a blast, look at him…" she waved her hand in Lee's direction. "… He's gorgeous, how could I not be happy? I think its when we attend events like this and everyone is talking about their kids and schools and little league and dance recitals, I get jealous, resentful and sad."

Paul hugged her again. "I know it's what you have always wanted Robin, but if I can give you a little advice, maybe you should just be happy with what you and Lee have and enjoy the ride your on. Man I'd be enjoying a ride anywhere on a Harley! Just think of how many people right here tonight feel jealous, resentful and sad at the life you have and they don't!"

Robin nodded her head. She understood what he was saying.

"Come on lets dance!" he said as he grabbed her hand and they went to dance to one of Rocket Fuel's number one hits.

Chapter Six

The band played for just over an hour, took a quick break, then went back on stage for another set. Robin had danced with Paul and then gone back to the table with him to meet his wife. She talked to Don while she was there. She didn't want to, but Paul convinced her that it would make her feel better if she just faced him. So she sat down at the table. She had had a few glasses of wine so she was a little more relaxed when she faced Don. He remained sitting, said hello then introduced his date "Joanne" as his girlfriend.

"Well Robin, you have really done ok for yourself." Don said quietly.

"Thank you. How have you been Don?" she asked sincerely.

"Okay I guess. I've been divorced twice. I guess that doesn't surprise you though?" He looked at her and smiled.

"No," she smiled back, "it doesn't. But I see you haven't given up." Nodding towards his new woman.

"No, never!" They both laughed.

Robin made small talk by asking what he was doing now. He replied that he was the manager of his father's car dealership as his father had retired a few years back and wanted Don to take over. Robin laughed to herself. A glorified car salesman, how appropriate. He even looked the part. Bald on top, with the row of fringe above his ears. Overweight with a big beer belly. Wearing a poor quality suit that just didn't fit right, with a bright red tie. Robin wondered if the tie was meant to attract attention to him.

They chatted for awhile longer. Robin told him a little about where she lived and about her life on the road with Lee, without going into too much detail. It was odd, describing her life to him she thought. With Don she did want to rub it in, but it just wasn't in her nature to do so. So she stuck with the smallest of details and let it go. The band was finishing up so Robin excused herself and went backstage. They did two encores, and after the final song Robin went back on stage.

"How about another big thank-you round of applause for Rocket Fuel!"

The crowd went wild.

Robin beamed. "I hope you enjoyed the show. We sure enjoyed being here. Enjoy the rest of the night and the weekend!"

The curtain fell and the guys started helping the crew break down the equipment. Robin hugged them all and thanked them again while Lee had gone to shower and change. She went downstairs to the dressing room shower to meet her husband. When he came out she walked over and wrapped her arms around him and gave him a big hug and a very long kiss.

"Thank you" she said "You and the guys were great. I was so proud."

He wrapped his arms around her and kissed her back long and hard.

When they separated she smiled at him and said "I love you for doing this tonight."

"Later Babe," he winked "you can show me how much." Then he kissed the end of her nose and grabbed her hand and said "Lets go dance!"

Robin and Lee both loved to dance. They glided together like they were one. They didn't often get a chance to dance together though. They danced a couple of two steps and then a waltz and a few fast dances. When they finally sat down Lee ordered them each a beer. People started crowding around Lee asking for his autograph. He politely refused,

"Not tonight, not here. This is Robin's night."

And then before they knew it the night was over. Robin had enjoyed herself. She had seen some old friends and actually got to dance with her husband!

They were staying at The Grand Pacific hotel downtown with the rest of the band. Robin's girlfriends had all made offers for them to stay with them, but she wanted to spend some quiet time alone with Lee and not impose. While Robin and Lee were waiting for a cab, Pam and Sara came to ask if they wanted to join them and get a bite to eat.

"Sure" Lee answered. "Where are you going?"

When the cab came, they let it go to someone else and joined the others in Pam's mini van. Pam drove, as she was the only one who hadn't been drinking.

"Are you okay Pam? Your not too tired?" Robin asked, concerned.

Pam turned and looked at Robin and broke out laughing.

"Rob, this is me Pam you're talking to. The party animal. Oh how quickly they forget. Just because I'm pregnant doesn't mean I can't still have fun. Besides I'm starving!"

Everyone was laughing now. They drove into town and decided on Chinese food. There was a new place that Robin had never heard of and everyone said it was the latest place in town to eat. It was very small and crowded even at this time of night. They had to wait for a bit, but were finally able to get a table for six.

The girls all started talking about the other girls and how much weight that one had gained and how good this one looked and how so and so hadn't changed a bit. They talked about all the couples who were divorced and remarried, there sure were a lot! Lee ordered drinks for everyone and said he was picking up the tab. They ordered a huge amount of food and it was delicious. Conversations and laughter continued for a couple more hours. When they were done, Pam drove Robin and Lee to the hotel and they all exchanged hugs and kisses, and agreed to see each other the next day at the ball game.

Inside the hotel, Lee held Robin's hand through the foyer and onto the elevator. Once inside the elevator and alone, he leaned her up against the wall and kissed her all the way up to the penthouse suite. The doors opened and they walked to their room. Lee unlocked the door and picked Robin up and carried her to the bedroom. Before long their elegant clothes were strewn all over the bedroom floor and they were engrossed only in each other. Sex was wonderful between them. It always had been.

Chapter Seven

When Robin had decided to move to Texas, everyone was shocked.

"Why so far away?" was the most common question. She wasn't sure herself. It was just something she felt she was supposed to do. She applied to colleges and universities that offered business and chef programs. Her mother was a fabulous cook and Robin had learned a lot from her but she wanted to try something different. Her mother was so comfortable in the kitchen. Robin wasn't quite as comfortable yet, but she really enjoyed trying new recipes and different things that her mother wouldn't cook. So she thought maybe a different style of cooking might appeal to her. She also loved cowboys, country music, rodeos, horses, and farms. Texas sounded more exciting than any old prairie town she could have gone to in Canada. So off she went at the age of nineteen to Texas. She was accepted to Texas Technological College in Lubbock. She would have preferred another city further south, but this was a start. Lubbock was one of the smaller metropolitan centers in Texas and the weather was warm and dry most of the time. She had to study Texas history In order to be accepted, so before she even got there she was fascinated. There was so much history in this state. The Texas Rangers, the varying weather from one side of the state to the other, the tales of the Texans and the Mexicans. She learned a lot. Lubbock was also only about seventy miles away from the New Mexico border so she planned to get there sometime too. She was accepted into the Home Economics Program and studied hard. She had a small apartment close to school and she got a job in the grocery store down the street. She was homesick for quite awhile. She missed her family and friends. But any spare time she had she studied or wrote letters home. The people at the grocery store had got to know Robin and they took her under their wings. It was a Mom and Pop operation, a neighborhood market. Most of the people who shopped there lived close by. Robin had met another girl who also worked there. Her name was Karen. She was going to high school, grade twelve, she would graduate this year. Robin helped her study and Karen introduced Robin to some of her friends. Although Robin was only nineteen, she was a real knockout and looked much older than she was. The fact that the drinking age was 21 didn't affect her. She would buy her new group of friends booze from time to time, but they would never do it in the neighborhood. They would go on road trips or to a lake and she didn't like to do it often, because if she got caught she could be in trouble and most likely get sent home to Victoria.

She went on dates with most of the guys who asked her out. She felt bad saying no. None of them she ever got too serious about. She was very skeptical of men ever since Don. So for now, she just wanted to have some fun, meet people and discover more about Texas. School was a real challenge, she had to study hard. She knew the fun and dating she had done in the summer had to stop. School, work and homework were all that Robin could fit into her life.

The first fall away from home was really tough. In Canada, Thanksgiving is the second Monday in October whereas in the United States it is in late November. Robin couldn't go home for the Canadian Thanksgiving and there was no point in going for the American as she would be going home a month later for Christmas. That first one was hard, but she was made to feel at home when the Arnold's, (the family who owned the grocery store) invited her to have Thanksgiving with them. She had offered to work extra hours over the weekend. So she ran the store with help from Karen and had a wonderful Turkey dinner with the Arnold's. She went home for Christmas and had a great visit with her family and Pam, Sara and Paul. They still could not understand why she had wanted to move to Texas. And she still really could not explain it. She wasn't sure she understood herself. It was something she knew she just had to do. And where she had to go. Her parents were very supportive of her, however they missed her terribly.

Robin had a younger brother Eddie. He was six years younger than she was. She actually missed him a lot and he missed her. They were never really close but they never really fought much either. Their age difference was most of the reason for the way they felt about each other. They knew they were family and they had a bond.

The summer of the first year in Texas, Robin wanted to go home, but she also had to work. She was going to have a heavy year next year, and was not going to be able to work as much as she should, so she would have to make extra money over the summer. She continued at Arnold's grocery store and got another job in a little gift shop on Sundays. Her life consisted of working days Monday to Friday at the grocery store, Saturday's off and working at the gift shop on Sundays. Her one night to go out was Friday. And she went out as often as she could. She was now twenty years old. At school she had met a guy named Jeff. He was from California and was an engineering student. They went on dates quite often and after awhile he asked her to go steady. She accepted. Jeff worked at a home building supply shop, which helped with his choice of education. He was a great guy and Robin enjoyed his company. She knew however in her heart that he was not the guy she was going to spend the rest of her life with. They got very intimate and Jeff was the first guy since Don that Robin had sex with. Robin was very cautious, but she realized that she was now older and could enjoy this if she wanted to. He was much gentler than Don was, and it was much more pleasant for Robin. She kind of liked it! She discovered that sex was an enjoyable experience. They dated that school year and when summer came, Jeff decided to move back to California and he wanted Robin to go with him. He begged and pleaded with her, and even proposed marriage. Robin loved Texas and was happy there, she liked her friends, and neighbors and her job. She didn't want to leave. Jeff was hurt and Robin was sad that the relationship ended, but she knew Texas was where she needed to be.

However, she had completed her basic home economics classes and a beginning chef course and now had to move to another university to take her practicum in Southwest cooking. She moved to Texas Southern University in Houston. What a place! It was close to the ocean. That was something Robin had really missed, the ocean! Victoria, where she grew up, is a city on Vancouver Island. A small island in the Pacific Ocean in Canada. Robin had lived almost nineteen years of her life surrounded by the ocean. As a small child her family would have picnics at the beach. They would go camping in the summer to the beach. Even in the winter, especially on a stormy day, they would go to the beach to watch the waves crash. Now she was close to the beach again. Galveston Bay, The Gulf of Mexico. Right there. This was going to be great living this close after having missed it for so long. Not only was the ocean close, so was NASA. Houston was also the largest city in Texas. She knew she would like it here.

Robin got set up for the next term at the university. She already knew she was accepted, but she had to find a place to live and a job. She checked in at the University housing office to see if they had any information as to finding a place to live. They gave her a list of places to call. Robin went through the list and found a small one-bedroom apartment in an old house that had been converted to suites. There were six apartments in the building and it was a quick walk to the university, so she took it.

The next day's task was to find a job just as close! She set about looking two days later. She had spent the previous two days setting up house. She was very happy and had met a few of her neighbors and they seemed pleasant. She had hoped that being a city as big as Houston, work would be plentiful, but the reality was that living this close to a University meant there were even more people looking for work. The Arnold's had given Robin an excellent reference, so had Mrs. Cumberland from the gift shop. Because she had studied as a chef and had completed the basic training, Robin was hoping to find a restaurant to work in. She made inquires at all the restaurants close to home and then realized that most students would not be eating at fancy restaurants, so there were not many nice ones close to school. She decided she would have to go a little further away to find what she was looking for. She finally found it. 'The Sunset Café.' It was perfect, not too big, not too small, not too expensive, but not cheap either. The menu looked delicious. Robin wanted to stay and eat but really had to get a job. She asked to speak with the owner. The lady who came to speak with Robin was about thirty-five years old and introduced herself as Maria. She went on to explain that herself and her husband Jose were the owners. Robin asked if there was any work and presented her letters of reference and showed Maria her grades from school. Maria hired her right on the spot saying she had never done that before. Usually her and Jose discussed everything, but she had a good feeling about Robin and wanted her to work there. She wanted Robin to start work that night. Robin happily agreed to. She then went home, puttered around her apartment, had a shower, braided her hair and returned to 'The Sunset Café!'

Chapter Eight

What a night! Robin and Lee had slept in the next morning, then they ordered room service for breakfast. As they waited for their food to arrive, lying embraced in each other's arms, Robin thanked Lee again for the wonderful evening the night before.

"You know Lee, I've never been so proud, I'm not sure if proud is the right word, but just plain thrilled to be your wife. Last night I felt so good and I was so happy to be coming home, being who we are. I owe it all to you. Thank you." She paused. "Do you think that I'm being catty or a bitch about this, thinking this way? And feeling this damned good?"

He kissed her forehead and said "You're welcome." Then he held her face with both of his hands and looked her in the eye, "No you are not being a bitch. You have every right to feel this damned good Robin. Look what you gave up to be married to me. You have worked just as hard as I have to get us to where we are today and quite frankly, I wouldn't be where I am if you hadn't been the type of wife you are. I owe you a lot and I'm dammed proud that you are my wife and you've stood beside me through the rough times as well as the good and God knows we've seen some rough times. If I can do anything to make you feel good and happy and proud and excited and thrilled, I will Robin, and I don't ever want you to forget it." Robin snuggled in under Lee's arm feeling very secure and loved. "Now shall we get to the ballgame?" he asked.

"No, not yet. I just want to stay here like this with you for awhile longer." She smiled and ran her fingers through the hair on his chest. Lee kissed her forehead again. There was a knock on the door, room service. Lee climbed out of bed and pulled a pair of jeans over his naked body and answered the door. After tipping the bellboy he wheeled the cart to the bed. "Your breakfast Madame" he announced in a very bad English accent with that fabulous smile on his face. Robin giggled and threw back the covers to expose her naked body and asked "Would you care to join me sir?" Without hesitation, Lee jumped on the bed and started tickling and kissing and hugging and before long, breakfast was getting cold.

All of a sudden they realized it was close to noon and they were supposed to be at the ballpark at eleven a.m. They ate the cold breakfast and packed up real fast. They had to check out of the hotel as they were catching a ten-forty-five p.m. flight to Vancouver, then a direct charter flight back to Houston. Robin put on a pair of jeans and a baseball shirt with "The Cotton's Honkey Tonk Bar and Grill" logo on it. She pulled her hair into a ponytail and pulled on a "Rocket Fuel" baseball cap. She tied up her runners and grabbed a jean jacket with the same logo as her ball cap. Lee was dressed almost the same. The only difference being Robin's shirt was blue, Lee's was black. Lee didn't put his hair into a ponytail, he just pulled the ball cap on backwards. They both put on sunglasses and grabbed their suitcases and headed for the elevator. They checked out and loaded their gear into the Ford Mustang they had rented for the weekend after the Harley was sent home on the semi with the band equipment.

It was now twelve-twenty, and they had to drive to the ball

diamond, which was about twenty minutes from where they were in downtown Victoria. It was a lovely fall day and Lee decided to put the top down on the car. It was refreshing. As they drove off, looking very much like the celebrities they were, Robin found a country station on the radio playing Garth Brook's "Calling Baton Rouge" and her and Lee held hands as they drove out to the country to play ball.

When they arrived at Layritz Ball Park, a park Robin herself had played little league at when she was seven and eight, of course the game was already in progress. Everyone started clapping and whistling. By this time Robin had hoped that they would not have to play and could maybe just watch. Not that she didn't like baseball, she loved it. But coming in late she didn't want to have special treatment or bump someone else out of a position. But both teams wanted both of them, so they each went to a different team. Lee grabbed Robin's arm and kissed her "Good Luck Babe!" he grinned and patted her behind as she ran to her dugout and he went to his. Robin's team put her out in left field, which was fine with her. She was so tired from the events leading up to this weekend. The planning, the trip up on the bike, the late nights and the fact that when they got home Lee would be leaving two days later for a three month tour. And this time Robin wouldn't be going with him. There was just too much to do at home. Perhaps that was what was so draining, she thought. She had gone on almost every road trip the last few years, ever since..............Robin didn't want to remember, but deep down inside she knew this was what she had been worrying about these past few weeks.

Chapter Nine

Robin took an instant liking to Jose and Maria and they to her. Her first night at the restaurant was pretty quiet. It was a Wednesday. 'Wicked Wednesday' they called it. Wednesday was the day they doubled up on the spices. Everything was hot, hot, hot. They served 'Blazing Bean Soup', 'Three pepper bread' and the main course, 'Habanero-Jalapeno chicken casserole'. Even the dessert was hot. The drink of the night was called a 'Wicked Woman'. Robin enjoyed the diversion from regular restaurant cooking. It was fun here, and a lot of work. Everything was prepared fresh each day. That first night Robin mainly observed Jose's style and Maria's watchful eyes. She checked everything before it left the kitchen. She was a stickler for perfection and presentation. Although this was just a small restaurant, Maria had big expectations. That first night Robin took it all in and was truly amazed that Maria had hired her on the spot. She could tell by Maria's presence in the kitchen that she was a perfectionist. Robin helped where she could and helped clean up the kitchen at the end of the night. They then started to do some prep for the next day. Jose went over the menu for 'Tequila Thursday' with Robin.

She was excited about coming back the next day. When she left the restaurant that night, she felt good and happy. She knew this job was the right one. It was really going to help her with her studies this term as well as be a fun place. Between school and work Robin would not have much of a social life.

"Good night Jose. Good night Maria. See you tomorrow. Thanks for a great first night!" Robin smiled as she walked through the door Jose held open for her.

"Good night Robin. I hope we didn't overwhelm you tonight." Maria said as she followed out the door.

"Oh no!" exclaimed Robin. "It was fun. I can't wait until 'Tequila Thursday' tomorrow."

"Well rest up dear, Thursday is our busiest night of the week. See you then."

Robin walked to her car, opened the door and climbed in. She headed for home. Although she wasn't tired at all it was half past midnight and she had to get up early in the morning to go and get all her books from the University bookstore as well as some last minute school supplies. When she got home and opened the fridge to grab a glass of milk she realized she would have to fit in grocery shopping as well. School would be starting next week and she would like to start being somewhat organized. Robin didn't have a television so she took her milk and turned the radio on low, opened the door to the small balcony off of her bedroom, then went outside and drank her milk looking up at the huge Texas sky.

The next morning, Robin was up by eight, dressed and out the door by eight forty-five. She walked to the university and had to wait in line to get into the bookstore. It would open at nine, and already the line was about forty people deep. She made idle chat with the girl in front of her, who had moved from Pennsylvania and was studying political science, something Robin was not interested in at all. Finally the doors opened and Robin had another line to wait in to get the home economic books she needed. Altogether Robin had spent almost two hours in lines at the bookstore but hopefully she was now ready for school. Robin walked back home and unloaded her bags of books and placed them together with all of the rest of her school supplies. She was hungry and opened the fridge and doing so remembered that there wasn't much there to eat so she decided to go and get some food.

This time she took her car and drove around the neighborhood. She drove up and down side streets and back streets just to get a feel for what was around her. She found a strip mall with a grocery store. This would do for today. It was close to home and she could even walk here if she didn't need too much. She went inside and as she started shopping she realized that she needed quite a few things. She got the basics, milk, bread, tea, lunch meats some fruit, she would be eating dinner at the restaurant most nights so all she really needed was breakfast, lunch and snacks.

When she got home she put away the groceries and made herself a sandwich. The weather was beautiful so she went out on the balcony to eat. After eating she lay down and let the warm sun beat down on her body. "Oh how good the sun feels" she thought to herself. "This is the first time I have actually sat down and relaxed since before I moved. It feels so good." She lay there dozing in the sun until three o'clock. When she looked at her watch she jumped up. She had to be at work at four. She jumped in the shower she didn't wash her hair, it would take too long. So she piled it into a bun on the top of her head, put on her makeup, changed into the white chef's uniform and headed off to work.

On her way to work, she was wondering what 'Tequila Thursdays' would be like. She arrived to work at three fifty three. She ran in, put on fresh lipstick washed her hands and got busy helping Jose chop vegetables.

"Are you ready for tonight?" Jose enquired with a smirk on his face while he de-boned a chicken.

"What's going to be happening here tonight?" Robin questioned back.

"Well senorita let me tell you. Cheap Tequila makes everyone crazy. They drink a lot, I sell them food. You see they can't drink here unless they eat a dinner, so we sell lots of food and lots of Tequila." He laughed.

"And you will see the crowd that comes in, they are about your age Robin, maybe you can meet some new people and make some friends in this city. There are a lot of regular 'Tequila Thursday' customers. I will introduce you to my favorites, ok?"

"Ok." Robin replied doubtfully.

True to his word, the restaurant was packed by six o'clock. Most of the crowd was in fact about Robin's age, which was now twenty-one. They were still pretty calm. Most of them were on their first drink. Robin was excited about working with a crowd like this. The music was playing. It was a party atmosphere and everyone was pretty happy. Robin and Jose were pumping the meals out as fast as they could with Maria doing her best at 'quality control' and helping to wait on tables. They had a bartender and two extra waitresses come in on Thursdays, Fridays, and Saturdays. All of whom Robin had not yet met.

It was nine o'clock and most of the six o'clock crowd had left to continue partying elsewhere. Now a whole new crowd was just starting to arrive. Jose brought Robin and himself in a tequila shooter.

"To get us through the next set of meals. Cheers!" and down it went.

Robin was hesitant, but Jose encouraged her and handed her a slice of lime.

"Cheers!" she said saluting with her glass and down hers went.

"Ahhh. That warmed the whole body." She laughed as she shuddered, chewing on the slice of lime.

"I'm proud of you Robin. No one else who has worked here has ever done that as well. They usually just sip on it, make it last all night. Maybe they are afraid to drink with the boss eh? What do you think?"

"Well I'm embarrassed now Jose. I guess I should have been more of a lady. The truth is," she looked around and whispered, "I really like Tequila."

Jose burst out laughing and slapped Robin on the back, "Oh I'm gonna love having you to work with. Maria had very good judgement this time. Let's go see who's out in the restaurant eh?"

Jose held open the kitchen door and together they went out to the dining room. The place was full. The restaurant was many levels, being in an older building with stairs and different sections all over the place. When it was full it sat about one hundred people. The décor was very Mexican with lots of plants, and terra cotta tile, blues, yellows and reds. A very bright, cheery room. Maria was scuttling about checking with people to see how everything was and clearing tables.

"There is a group of people who have been coming in here every Thursday for a couple of years. They play in a band, and usually they play at the bar around the corner on Friday and Saturday nights. They are our best customers. They have brought in a lot of business for us. So every week we reserve the upper level for them. I would like you to meet them, they will help you meet new people here." Jose continued walking through the restaurant saying hello to people as he walked, stopping here and there to shake someone's hand and to introduce Robin. When they reached the upper level Robin saw a table of about fifteen people enjoying themselves. They were all about Robin's age she figured, and looked pretty cool.

"Hello my friends!" Jose exclaimed as he gave hugs to everyone at the table.

"Welcome back. Welcome my friends. I have someone I would like you all to meet." He then grabbed Robin's hand and pulled her closer to the table.

"This my friends is Robin. She is my new chef and she likes to drink Tequila!" He laughed and the whole table started laughing with him. Robin felt her face go fifty shades of red. She was so embarrassed. She hung her head trying to hide her face, but looked up to smile and say,

"Hello."

"Robin has just moved here from Lubbock and before that she came from Canada. I would like you all to be friends. She doesn't know anyone here. She goes to the University to get more cooking papers, although I don't think she needs them." He patted Robin on the back.

"Thank-you Jose. It's very nice to meet you. I would like to get to know all of you better, but right now there isn't anyone in the kitchen and I'm sure if Maria finds out I will be out of a job as fast as I got one." They all broke out in laughter.

"I hope to get a chance to meet y'all again soon. I have to get back to work now." She waved and made her way back to the kitchen alone. Jose stayed to have a shot of Tequila and visit with his friends.

The rest of the evening went very quickly. It was so busy. Robin was cleaning up the kitchen and getting pots and utensils ready for the next day. It was twelve-twenty a.m. Jose had come back to help finish the cooking but he left again to let Robin do the clean up alone. The waitresses, Suzanne and Sandy, who Robin had now been introduced to, were running the dishes through the dishwasher, filling up condiment bottles and folding napkins for tomorrow. They were only about seventeen or eighteen Robin figured by their conversations. The bartender's name was Martin. He seemed friendly and was polite and was probably about the same age as Jose and Maria, mid thirties Robin guessed. Robin was almost finished when Jose came in. She could tell that he had had a few too many shots of tequila.

"My new friend Robin," he chortled as he came and put his hand on Robin's back. "My other friends would like to meet you now. Can you come? Leave all this, I will do it tomorrow, it is late now, you must relax."

Robin didn't know what to say. So she washed her hands and went to check how she looked in the mirror. She put on some new lipstick and straightened some straggling hairs and undid the top button of her chef's whites.

"Ok let's go!" She smiled as Jose led her back up to the top level. He stopped at the bar and grabbed a bottle of Cuervo to take with them. When they got to the table, there were only three guys left. Jose held out a chair for Robin and introduced her to them.

"Robin, this is Joe, this is Billy, and this is Lee. I hope you will all be friends." Robin shook each of their hands and said hello again. Jose poured each of them a shot of Tequila, cut up a new lime and handed each of them a slice.

"Boy, how many of these have you guys had?" Robin asked pointing to a pile of lime rinds and a stack of empty shot glasses.

"Only a couple," answered the fellow named Billy.

"Those are all from everyone else who was here earlier." They all started laughing.

"Don't lie to the lady," said the guy named Lee, "but we've only had a couple.....of bottles that is!" They all started laughing again. "You better catch up Robin."

With that, she took her glass, shot it and chewed on the lime.

"How many am I going to have to have to drink to catch up?" She asked with a grin on her face. She was sitting beside the fellow named Lee. He was quite good looking, with nice curly chin length dirty blonde hair, great blue eyes, and a fabulous smile. It seemed he was tall and he looked a tad on the skinny side.

"Oh about a dozen more." Lee answered staring directly into Robin's eyes.

She looked directly back at him with her eyes popping out of her head,

"I don't think so! I wouldn't make it to work tomorrow if I did that. Besides it's 'Fresh Friday' tomorrow and I don't want to miss that!"

"We usually miss it." Replied Joe. "We're in a band and we usually have gigs on Friday and Saturday nights. Sometimes we come late on Saturday and Jose stays open for us. We don't like to miss his 'Seafood Saturdays'."

"What kind of music do you guys play?" Robin asked. She suddenly realized that she and Lee still hadn't released each other's gaze and that the Mexican/Caribbean music that had been playing all night was now silent.

"Were a little of a lot of kinds." Lee responded, "some rock, blues, disco, dance type, lots of old rock, we try to keep up with the new stuff, but mostly we play whatever people will dance to."

"I'd love to hear you sometime. I haven't been dancing for a very long time." Robin stated, looking back at Lee while she was talking. He smiled at her and she got that warm fuzzy feeling like she had known him forever.

"Well if your boss ever gives you a Friday or Saturday off, let me know, I can let you know where we will be playing." He poked at Jose who laughed and said " I don't know if I should let my Robin get mixed up with you guys. All you do is break women's hearts. You have a new one every week! I can't have her in my kitchen crying about one of you and then you will take all your business to another restaurant. Oh no! I think I have done a bad thing by introducing you to this pretty young girl who comes to work for me. You better not hurt her, any of you!" he said pointing a finger at each of them. They all just laughed at him and said as soberly as they could, "Yes Dad!"

"Well on that note, I think I had better get home. I'm not sure what to expect tomorrow after tonight." Robin said standing.

"Do you need a ride?" Lee asked.

"Oh no thanks. I have my car and I don't live far. Thanks anyway. Hope to see you again sometime." She started to walk away and quickly turned back.

"Actually, do you need a ride? I haven't been drinking as much as you guys." She had to peel her gaze away from Lee's to see what the response was from the rest of the guys.

"No, no we're ok." said Billy and Joe in unison. "We all came together." added Joe.

"Well if you don't mind, I would much rather get a ride home with a pretty lady than with you guys. I'll take you up on your offer. If it's ok with you Jose?" Lee stood smiling at Robin then glanced at Jose for his approval.

"You break her heart, I kill you! Okay?"

"Ok deal!" Lee shook Jose's hand, paid his bill, grabbed his jacket and said goodnight to the guys.

"Robin you tell me if he's not good to you Okay? See you tomorrow."

"Good night Jose. Good night Billy, Good night Joe, nice to meet you."

Chapter Ten

Crrrraaakk! Robin had to snap back to attention, the ball was coming right out in left field, and it was her husband who had hit it. Fortunately it was a fly ball so she basically just had to stand there and let it fall into her glove. It did. Everyone yelled and clapped and whistled. Lee made a disappointed face and yelled out to Robin, "I'll get you later for that Sweetheart!"

That was two out, one more to go and the game would be over. In a few hours they would be heading home and all this fun and togetherness would be over. Lee would be back to work and Robin would be 'burning the home fires'. Third out. Back to the dugout.

The game was over and everyone headed for the beer and barbecue set up at the side of the park. Robin talked to a few people she couldn't really remember. She recognized their faces but didn't remember their names. That was uncomfortable but she was actually really good at making conversation with people she didn't know. Being Lee's wife, she had to do at a lot. When she was working in the bar at home she talked to customers all the time and was very courteous and polite. Even when she didn't know who the heck they were. But this was different, she should know these people, after all, she spent a couple of years at least with some of them. Paul and his wife came over to talk and Robin reintroduced Lee to Paul, but his wife, Sandy, had not yet met Lee, so Robin introduced them. Paul shook Lee's hand and said "Well, I see you've been taking good care of her Lee, she looks great and happy. I won't have to beat you up this trip." Paul lightly patted Lee's back. They all laughed.

"Yeah she's doing okay Paul. I hope you're not disappointed you don't have to keep me in line this time. I've been known to need keeping in line from time to time." Lee glared at Robin with a goofy face that only she would understand.

"Yes he has! And I'm not doing it anymore. He's big and ugly enough to look after himself these days. Besides I have too much other stuff to do. He's going on the road for three months two days after we get home and I'm not going this time so he'd better behave himself or I will call you Paul and have you take a round out of him." Then Robin punched Lee's shoulder and they all started laughing again.

"Wow, three months away. That must be tough!" Sandy commented.

"Well after seventeen years, I'm kind of getting used to it." Robin lied. She would never get used to it. She didn't mind the fact that Lee's work took him on the road. It was just all the damned women and all the attention. It would be ok if he didn't get so involved with the fans, but that was part of the job. Robin was the one who needed to deal with it.

"Come on let's go get another beer and let these guys talk."

Robin and Sandy went and stood in the beer line and decided to get burgers while they were there. Sara and Glenn came over and said they were going home to get their kids and would be back in half an hour.

"Please Robin don't leave until the kids see you. They will be so disappointed if they miss you this visit."

"I'm not going anywhere. We have already checked out of the hotel and we don't need to be to the airport until around nine-thirty. We've got lots of time to kill. We'll stay until you get back. Hurry, I'm dying to see my godchildren!"

The girls got the beer and burgers and went back to where Lee and Paul were sitting.

"Well have you guys had a good visit?"

"Yeah we have. Paul's been telling me all about his work. And it sounds great. Next time we're home I want to see him in action." Paul was the manager at the local brewery.

Robin turned to Lee and said, "Sara and Glenn have just gone to get the kids, and they would like us to stick around until they get back."

"No problem. There's lots of food, lots of beer. I'm happy."

Pam and Marty came and joined the group and before long Sara and Glenn were back so they all ate dinner together. Robin took the kids to the car to get them the small gifts she had bought for them. And the gift for Travis, Pam's son who had spent the weekend at his grandparents house. The kids both got tussled up by Uncle Lee. They thought that was great. Then they proceeded to tell him all the times they had seen him and the band on television. They told him how famous he was and could they get his autograph (again) to show their friends (again). Lee played the naïve star, "Who me? Famous? No way!"

"Yes Uncle Lee, we see you all the time on CMT!"

"Me on CMT, are you sure?"

"Yup we're sure!"

"Well if you're sure it's me, then I guess I'd better wave or say 'Hi' to you next time. What do you think?"

"Yes, Yes! Please say, 'Hi Tyler and Tiffany Amos'. Make sure you say Amos so we know you mean it for us."

"What about Aunt Robin, do you think she is famous too?"

"Well, no. We don't ever see her on CMT."

"You know what? Just cause she's not on TV doesn't mean she's not famous. I happen to think she is really famous just for being her. And you know what else I think? I think you guys are pretty famous too."

"Oh Uncle Lee, don't be silly, we're not famous."

"Yes you are. And don't you ever forget it! Your Mom and Dad think your famous and so do Auntie Robin and I."

"Tyler, Tiff, stop bugging Uncle Lee. Go play." Glenn intervened and sent the kids to the playground.

"Sorry Lee. They get pretty excited." He added.

"Hey, no problem. They are great kids."

Lee watched them go to the playground and took the last swig of his beer. He stood up and offered to go get another round. The guys all went together so it left the girls alone to chat.

"Rob, he's looking pretty hot! If I wasn't married and eight months pregnant.........."

"Yeah, you and half the world." Robin said sarcastically.

"Oh a little tense are we?"

"I'm sorry Pam." She reached over and held Pam's hand.

"He's leaving for a road trip in two days. I am just a little tense, tired and worried. I didn't mean to be so sarcastic. We have just had the best two weeks I think we've had for years. I don't mean that we don't have good times, we have the best times! Everyday I have to pinch myself to see if this is really my life. But this time we've been away from his work, until we got here that is. Then it was back to work. But on the way here we were just Robin and Lee and company. And even the rest of the guys were different. We all spend so much time together so you get to know each other real well and like I said they were all so relaxed and carefree. That's the word, carefree. I could feel it. I could see it. It was just so damned nice, and now it's going to end. When we are at home there is so much to do, we are always on the go. Oh I'm sorry you guys! I didn't mean to dump all my troubles on you. Here I come for a visit and what do I do but whine?"

"Robin, let it out girl. It sounds like you need a shoulder to cry on. Talk to us, we're still your friends even though were so far apart." Pam held on tight to Robin's hand and rubbed her back.

"I don't know what else to say. It's just been so nice and I don't want it to end yet. And I know, as soon as we get home I'll be fine. It really does bother me that he is so damn good looking. I just have to keep reminding myself that he is my husband and I am his wife and enjoy it. All the good, and the bad. Didn't we agree to something like that when we took our marriage vows?"

They all started laughing. The guys came back then with more beer. They sat around and took turns telling stories. The rest of the crowd was slowly leaving. Robin went and said goodbye to the organizers of the reunion and thanked them for inviting Lee and the band to sing. And for asking her to be the Master of Ceremonies.

"Well be back for our thirtieth. I can't wait. Thanks again."

It was now six o'clock. Everyone was leaving. Sara came and gave Robin a hug and looked her right in the eyes and said, "Robin, if you ever need to talk, please call me anytime. Please. I know we are a long way apart, but if I can ever help you please call."

"Yes, Sara. You too. You know, I'm not the only one who needs to talk. I'll call, I promise. Take care of those kids. Love y'all." Robin and Sara gave each other big hugs. Then Glenn and the kids came and said goodbye. Then Pam and Marty did the same.

"You know Robin, we get a discount to fly, so maybe after this kids born, I'll come and stay with you for awhile."

"Oh Pam would you?" I would love it. Anytime! You know, we've got plenty of room and two grandmothers with no grandchildren, so bring the baby. Oh Pam it would be fun. Bring the whole family. I would love to show you this new house and the ranch. Oh Pam, please let's plan it. I'll call you in a couple of weeks."

"Sure and if you need me in the meantime, you know how to get me." Pam reached out and gave Robin the best hug she could with her big belly in the way. They both giggled and wiped away tears.

"Thanks Pam, I love you. Take care."

Lee got hugs and handshakes all round also. Then they headed for the car.

"Well honey, a successful weekend I'd say."

"Do you think it went well Lee?"

"Yeah, I thought it was great. Everyone looked like they were having a good time."

"Robin, Robin" someone was calling. Robin turned. It was Don. He was signaling for her to come over to him.

"I'll wait in the car. I've got to put the top up so go ahead, I'll be here."

"Thanks Honey, I'll be right back." Robin walked over to where Don sat. She could tell before she even got near that he was drunk.

"Hi Don, how are you today?" She asked politely.

"Hi. I'm okay. Are you leaving?"

"Yes. We have to catch a flight to Vancouver then another to Texas."

"You know Robin, I never could figure out why you wanted to go to Texas. But I can see it hasn't hurt you. Do you really like it there?"

"Yes Don. I love it there. It's my home now and I am very happy there."

"Well I can see you married the right kind of guy. I guess you must love him 'cause he must have a lot of money."

"Well Don, I can see you are still the ass you've always been. I'm so glad I didn't marry you!"

"I wouldn't have married you! I just wanted to fuck you. And I did! And now I can tell everyone that I fucked Mr. Big Shot country star's wife!"

"Don, when you 'fucked' me, I wasn't anyone's wife. I was your girlfriend and I thought you gave a damn. But I sure was wrong wasn't I?

And besides if you knew how to 'fuck' maybe you wouldn't have been divorced so many times!" Robin started walking away.

"You Bitch! You think you're so high and mighty and have the most wonderful star for a husband. You really think you're somebody don't you? You come back here and rub it in all our faces. Flaunting all your money and Harley's and cars and clothes and jewelry."

"You've got a big problem pal. I love my husband very much and you know what makes me sick is that at one time I thought I loved you this much. But you could never compare to Lee. Never! And we have both worked, worked Don, you don't even know the meaning of the word do you? We've worked hard for every single thing we have and I'm proud to come back here and say look what I've done with my life. Unlike you who had Mommy and Daddy to look after him all his life. It really disgusts me that I ever knew a person as shallow as you. Get a life Don, before it's too late." With that said, Robin ran to the car in tears. She jumped in and told Lee to start the engine and get the hell outta there.

Chapter Eleven

Lee followed Robin to her car and opened her door for her.

"Thanks Mr........do you have a last name sir?"

"Well yes ma'am I do. It's Cotton. Lee Brodie Cotton at your service!"

"Mr. Cotton, would you like to join me for a carriage ride. I promise I won't turn into a pumpkin as it's already after midnight."

"Very well ma'am. But you don't know what I might turn into!" They both started laughing. Lee ran around and got in the passenger side. Robin started the engine and put in an Eagles tape.

"So Mr. Cotton where abouts in Texas do you live? This is a huge place, I could be driving for days."

"Only a couple of miles away actually. Over on Elm, by the university."

"I live close to the university too, on Spruce St. How far apart are Elm and Spruce?"

"Well, there's Elm, Cedar, Oak, Fir, then I think Spruce or maybe Maple. Anyway we must live close to each other."

"Do you go to the university?"

"That's a long story. You wanna hear it?"

"Sure, I've got nothing to do until four o'clock tomorrow afternoon!"

"I started going to school two terms ago. Taking a major in music. Myself, and a few guys who I had been friends with in high school, had started a band. We mostly played school dances and at parties for our friends. When I started university, I had a real heavy load and I had to stop the gigs because it took so much time to practice new material and I write songs too. I just couldn't find time to do it all and hold down a job. I worked pumping gas on the weekends. That in itself was tough. I would be up all night Friday doing a gig somewhere. And afterwards you can't calm down, you're just flying so we would go to an all night restaurant, chow down and drink coffee. Then I would go home and have a shower and try to read or do something to calm down. But I had just finished drinking a million cups of coffee. So I would turn on the TV and fall asleep in front of it for a couple of hours. Then get up for work at seven a.m., work till four p.m., go home, shower, grab some food and do it all over again. I quit for a year then met some guys at University who wanted me to play with them so I did occasionally. Then one day I realized I missed the stage and singing and the lights and the crowds, but most of all the music. It's my life. All I've ever wanted to do is play music and sing and perform. So I quit school and have been playing the bar circuit ever since."

"Excuse me, but where are we going?"

"Do you feel like going home yet?"

"No actually, not really. I'd like to hear more about your life. What do you want to do? I can take you home if you'd like."
"No I'm a night owl. So I'm not ready to go home yet. Let's see. Do you know how to get to the beach?"

"The beach? Is it close? I would love to go to the beach! You would not believe how much I miss it! Which way?"

"Slow down darlin'. It will take about an hour to get there.

More or less. Do you want to change or just go like that?" Lee pointed to her dirty chef's whites.

"Oh yeah. I would love to change." They drove to Robin's house. Lee came in and sat on her couch to wait. Looking around the room, he noticed she didn't have a TV. "I can't believe it no TV?" he yelled to Robin. "How do you watch Dallas?"

"I don't. Besides when school starts I don't have time. You know what I mean?" She came walking out of her bedroom wearing jeans and a pink blouse. Brushing out the shoulder length blonde hair she had just let out of the bun that she had put it in for work. Lee took a second glance. She was stunning. She didn't look like the same girl he walked in there with. She looked much thinner out of her work clothes and her hair was beautiful. It set off the blue of her eyes, which he noticed, sparkled when she smiled.

"Wow, you look different!" he grinned.

"Oh is that good or bad?" she asked very self-consciously.

"Good, good. You look great. Not what I pictured you would look like with your hair down and clothes on."

"What?"

"That's not what I mean. Well it is what I mean. Do you know what I mean?"

Robin started giggling.

"I hope it means that you think I look better than you thought I would."

"Yes, that's exactly what I mean. Thank-you. I hope you didn't take it any other way."

"Well I was wondering there for a second or two. Do you know that it's two o'clock in the morning? I'm really tired after working tonight. I was wondering if we could just have a cup of coffee and I could have a rain check on the beach?"

"Would you like me to leave?"

"Oh no, not at all. I just realized what time it was and how long it would take us to get there and back and I think I would just like to sit down and relax a bit. Ok with you? Coffee?"

"Sure, coffee sounds great. Can I help?" He followed Robin to the kitchen and leaned on the counter as she filled the kettle and turned on the stove. She pulled the coffee out of the cupboard.

"I hope instant's ok. It's decaf. Or I have tea."

"The decaf is fine."

"Go sit down. I'll get some food and be right there."

Lee walked back to the living room and settled in on the sofa. Robin got mugs out of the cupboard. She found some cheese and crackers and put them on a plate. She looked out at Lee sitting on her couch and thought to herself,' I'm so glad we didn't go to the beach. God Robin you don't even know this guy. Yeah, but look at him! He is very cute and he seems nice enough and Jose knows him. Don't be nervous, go out there and get to know him. The funny thing was that Robin didn't feel nervous. She felt comfortable with this guy and she felt like she already knew him.

They stayed up all night long talking. Robin learned that Lee's father worked at NASA. His mother stayed at home. He had two brothers, he was born in Dallas, and he was twenty-three years old. The family moved to Houston in 1963 and he has played in bars all over the state of Texas. He loves to travel. Lives with Bo and Billy in the house on Elm St. they are brothers and their father owns the house and charges them really cheap rent. He drives a 1969 Ford pickup truck, is single at the moment, he thinks.

"Wait a minute. What do you mean you think?" Robin questioned.

"Well I was sort of dating this girl, Debbie. And she was getting mad because we could never go on a date or make plans for the weekend together cause I'm always working. She was getting tired of waiting around for me all night. I don't blame her, but it's my job, that's what I do. I have to work. I have bills and rent and this is what I want to do for the rest of my life. If she can't understand that then I guess she's not the right girl for me. Anyway, does that sound cold and uncaring, or selfish to you Robin?"

"Not really. I can understand her feelings. If she's got a boyfriend she would like to spend time with him and do things with him. But I also understand your point of view, and I know exactly what you mean. It's the same for me, remember?

He nodded his head.

"I have no choice either. I have to work, I have to go to school which means studying, lots of it. And if I have someone who understands my life and can live with it, that's great. But most people can't live with it. That's why I'm single."

Lee asked "Do you have anyone who's like Debbie, sitting around waiting for you?"

"No. Not anymore. I had a great boyfriend in Lubbock. But he wanted to go back to California and wanted me to go with him. But you know what? I didn't feel it was right. He was a wonderful person and treated me great, but he didn't understand why I wanted to go to school and study 'cooking'. He couldn't get the fact that that was more important to me than he was. And I really love Texas. I don't want to leave. I think I will be here for the rest of my life."

"Finally, someone who understands!" They both started laughing.

"Miss.........what's your last name Robin?"

"Dean"

"And a middle name?"

"Suzanna. Robin Suzanna, after my grandmother, Dean."

"Miss Dean, would your carriage mind giving this tired guy a ride home?"

"No not at all. Let's go." They got up and Robin grabbed a sweater and her purse and off they went. The ride was quick, they were only four blocks apart.

"Would you like to come in and see my place?"

"Maybe some other time thanks."

"I hope that's not like, 'I'll call sometime'." Lee was serious.

Robin laughed. Now she was feeling nervous.

"No it's just late and we need to get some sleep and besides you owe me a raincheck for the beach. Don't forget."

"Would you like to go this Sunday? Maybe Jose will give you the night off."

"I don't work Sunday, Monday, or Tuesday this week, so that would be great."

"Ok then. I will probably see you late Saturday night. Will you still be at the restaurant?"

"Sure. I'll stay until you come."

"It's been a pleasure meeting you Robin. Thanks for the ride." He leaned over and kissed Robin right on the lips.

"Hmmm, that was nice."

Then he put his arm around her shoulder and leaned in for another.

"Do you mind?" He asked, as he looked her straight in the eyes. She was speechless. She just looked into his eyes and slightly nodded her head. He kissed her again this time with some power and some passion. Robin felt her whole body tingle, even her toes were tingling. She had never been kissed like that before. Not ever. It seemed like it lasted forever and Robin was sure she was in heaven. She opened her eyes as he moved away from her.

"I've got to go. Thanks again for the ride." He jumped out of the car and ran to the house turning to wave as he went through the front door. Robin couldn't see, but he got inside and jumped in the air and yelled,

"Whooo eeeee. I've found the woman of my dreams!"

Robin sat in the car for a few moments before she regained her composure. She was numb on the short drive home. She parked the car and went inside. Her whole body was still tingling. 'Wow' was all she could say. She got ready for bed but was so enamoured, it took two hours before she fell asleep.

When she got up she was anticipating her night at work. It didn't matter anymore that it was 'Fresh Friday', she just wanted

'Seafood Saturday' to get there quick. She got to work at three-forty-five and began to do some prep work in the kitchen. Jose had already done most of it. Dinner was a huge salad bar with just the regular restaurant menu tonight. Robin played around with a few salad dressing combinations and finally came up with one she was pleased with. The drink specials tonight were 'Fresh Fruit Daiquiris' and 'Fresh Fruit Margaritas'. The evening went very smoothly and the place wasn't quite as busy as the night before. When they had a quiet moment Jose brought Robin a Margarita and asked how her date with Lee went.

"Jose, how well do you know Lee?"

"I know him for three, maybe two years. He nice guy. Give good tip, very polite." Robin noticed, for the first time that Jose's English sounded better the more he had to drink. Since this was his first of the evening, he was still being cautious with his wording.

"Do you know if he has a girlfriend?"

"Oohh Robin, you fall for my friend Lee? Yes I can tell. I can see in your eyes!"

"Oh God! Is it that obvious? Jose we stayed up all night talking. I have never felt this way before. He kissed me goodnight and I melted right on the spot. I don't know how I can feel this way, I've only known him twenty-four hours. Is it possible?"

"Yes Robin. If two people are right for each other then anything is possible. I'm sure it can happen that fast, like love at first sight. I wonder how Lee feels about you?" He pointed at Robin and smiled. She blushed and looked down at the floor.

"I don't know. Please Jose, don't say anything to him or any of his friends. I would feel really embarrassed if he has a girlfriend. But, we're going on a date to the beach on Sunday and he said he would see me here late tomorrow night."

"My Robin, I feel good about this. I think you would be perfect for Lee and he would be good to you. I want to celebrate. Drink your drink and lets get back to work."

She gulped down the Margarita and continued with work.

The night was finally over and Robin couldn't wait to go home to bed.

She had just gotten into bed and it was about two-thirty a.m. when she heard a 'tap tap' at her door. Robin jumped up, put on her house-coat and went to answer it.

"Who is it?" She whispered loudly.

"It's me, Lee."

Robin slowly opened the door. Sure enough it was him.

"What are you doing here? Come on in."

She pulled the door open and he came in.

"Were you asleep?" he asked.

"No. I did just go to bed though. I have no makeup on, I must look horrible." She tried to cover her face with her hands.

"What are you doing here?" she asked again.

"I couldn't wait till tomorrow. I just wanted to come and say good night to you. I thought about you all night. You could never look horrible. I hope you don't mind. I just want a kiss good night.....if that's alright?"

"I thought about you all night too. Even Jose knew it."

Lee laughed "Yeah, he would. He can read me like a book."

"Well I've only known him a few days, how can he read me already?"

"He feels things and he just knows. Trust his judgement, he's usually right. How would you feel about that kiss?"

"I'm not used to being asked at this hour of the night for a kiss!" Robin said quietly, "but I'm sure I won't mind."

Lee stepped toward Robin and wrapped his arms around her and gazed right into her blue eyes and she felt herself melt even before he kissed her. Then the kiss came. His lips were soft and hot and hungry. Robin felt her arms go around Lee's neck, her hands were running fingers through his hair. They kissed kiss after kiss. His hands were caressing her back and had gotten inside her house-coat. It was open and all she had on was a short semi-sheer pink baby doll nightgown. His hands went up and down her back and rubbed her behind and finally found their way to her breasts. He moaned as he felt the firmness of what he found. He pulled away and said "I've got to go." He took another look at what he had revealed under the open house coat. "Oh God, I've really got to go."

He grabbed Robin once more and kissed her with so much passion then pulled away again. "I'll see you tomorrow." He kissed her one more time and left. Robin leaned up against the door in a state of delightful shock. She could still feel him holding her. In a daze she locked the door and went to bed. She had a wonderful sleep.

The next day she woke at one o'clock in the afternoon feeling so good. She knew that tonight would be interesting if Lee showed up after work. She hoped he would. She went shopping that afternoon and bought herself some nice lacy underwear and a matching sexy bra. She also bought a bottle of wine and a package of condoms. *Just in case!* She then went to the grocery store to get a few items, *just in case*, he stayed over and they would need breakfast. While she was there she picked up a six pack of beer, *just in case* he didn't drink wine. She rushed home, tidied up the place, had a shower, got into her work clothes and headed to the Sunset Café.

Chapter Twelve

It was almost four when Robin ran through the door, she hated being late, but today, time had just gotten away from her.

"Hello Robin. How are you today?" Jose asked as she ran past him to the kitchen.

"Nervous Jose, and apprehensive. How are you? What kind of night are we going to have tonight?"

"Robin don't be nervous. Just relax, take it easy. Enjoy tonight. The food is great, you will see." He followed her into the kitchen. Maria was in there putting finishing touches on pecan pies.

"Hello Robin. How are you today? Jose tells me you have met Lee. You be careful with that boy. He drinks too much and has new girlfriends all the time. I have to admit he is cute and if I was younger I might be interested in a boy like him. But he likes the fast life and parties. Robin, I just want to warn you so you don't get hurt." Maria turned and left the kitchen.

"Oh don't listen to that old stick in the mud. She doesn't know how to have fun. All she want to do is work, work, work. No drinking, no party, no fun. I think I only young once. Have fun! Lee and his friends are the closest I get to having any fun.

I look forward to seeing them every week, they make me realize what I missed out on. You see, Maria and I got married when she was fifteen and I was seventeen. Our families were poor so we worked doing all kinds of jobs just to get by and to help our families. She wouldn't even have any children because she says she doesn't want them to be poor like us. Do you know Robin, we now have lots of money and she is less fun than when we had nothing. She still just wants to work, work, work. That's why I like to see young people doing things and having fun while they can, you know before they get married and have an old stick in the mud to live with!" He laughed then said, "We better get to work or we will both be in trouble."

They both got busy preparing the specials of the night. 'Texas Boiled Shrimp' was the appetizer. 'Shrimp and chilies with sherry sauce', for the first main course. 'Abalone steaks' for the second. 'Crab Louis' for the salad. And Jose had made a huge pot of 'Cioppino' which had been simmering for a few hours. All that needed to be added was the seafood.

"Jose, this look fabulous. I can't wait to try your Cioppino. I hope there'll be some left later."

"Have some now Robin."

"No thanks. My stomach is doing flip flops right now." She made a silly face and continued to chop.

"I hope Maria has not upset you."

"No, no. I just get like this. I worry about everything. Especially when men are involved. I don't have very good luck in the love department!" She laughed and chopped a green pepper with the force you would use to chop a piece of wood.

"I should really avoid them, it would make my life a little simpler. You know, one less thing to worry about."

"Robin, I don't want you to worry about Lee. I can tell you are made for each other and everything will be fine. I will even bet that you two get married and have a big family. I can feel it. It feels right." He stared at Robin and patted his chest the entire time he was talking.

"Jose how can you say that, you don't even know me, I've only been here three days and already you've got me married and having kids with a guy I don't even know! Maybe I don't want to get married or have kids."

Robin was getting angry. "Jose all I want from here is a job that is fun and helps to pay my rent, and my bills and helps with my education. Beyond that I'm not ready to think about right now. So let's just take it day by day and see what happens, ok?"

"Ok. Robin I'm sorry." Jose walked over and hugged her.

After that, the night was very busy. The food poured out of the kitchen and was enjoyed by the consumers. The 'Man o War' was the drink special. A wild mix of Gin, Vodka, White Rum, mixed with Grenadine and 7-up with a shot of Crème de Cacao to make it look like a giant jellyfish. It was pretty disgusting looking, but quite a few were ordered. It was just past midnight and Jose came into the kitchen with a 'Man o War' for Robin and himself.

"Here's to a busy night. Thanks for making it go so smoothly. Cheers."

They both took a gulp.

"Jose, this is the worst drink I have ever tasted." Robin had a curled up face and was sucking on her lips. "Yuck, give me a shot of Tequila anytime over this shit."

Jose was killing himself laughing and pulled a bottle of Tequila out of a cupboard and two shot glasses out of his pocket.

"I knew you would say something like that." He poured each of them a shot. How are you feeling now, ready for some Cioppino?"

"Is there still some left?"

"Yes."

"What happens when Lee and the guys get here? Do they eat or just drink?"

"Both, but mostly drink."

"Should I wait and eat when they come or should I eat now?"

"Why don't we start to clean up. Then when they arrive you can sit down and eat with them and I will prepare whatever they want. Sound good?"

"Sounds great. But I want the Cioppino, don't let it all go."

They saluted each other again and downed the Tequila. Then got busy cleaning and putting food and dishes away. Before long it was one-forty five and Robin could hear it get louder in the restaurant. Jose went to look and came back with a smile on his face.

"They are all here Robin. Would you like to go sit with them now?"

"Was he with a girl?"

"There are girls out there but I don't know who they all belong to. Just go and sit and I will get the food ready."

Robin was really nervous. The Tequila hadn't helped yet. She went and checked out how she looked in the mirror, put on fresh lipstick, wiped her face with a damp paper towel, fixed her straggling hair and undid the top button of her uniform.

"Mind if I take another shot with me Jose?"

"Go ahead. Get out there."

Robin picked up the Cuervo bottle and filled her glass, then left the kitchen and walked to the back section of the restaurant where all the noise was coming from. It was the same table they were in the other night. She spotted Lee right away and didn't really notice anyone else. He stood up and walked over to her and gave her a quick kiss on the cheek.

"Hi Robin. I'm glad you're still here. It's great to see you again. How was your night?"

"Hi. It's great to see you again too. Although we must stop meeting in the middle of the night like this." They both laughed.

"Can't do much about that. At least we are both on the same schedule."

"That's true. My night's been great. Really busy, which was good. And the food is great. How was your night?"

"It was ok. We had a rowdy crowd tonight, must be a full moon or something. Come on let's sit down and I'll introduce you to everyone."

They both sat down and Lee did the introductions. Robin couldn't remember everyone's names. She did remember Joe and Billy from the other night, but she had already forgotten everyone else. She did notice however that there was no one named Debbie. Finally she could relax a bit. The waitress came and took everyone's orders. Robin excused herself to go help Jose with the food.

"No girlfriend that I can see." She beamed as she walked through the kitchen doors. "I'll help you Jose, that's a lot of food to prepare."

"Good news then eh? Ok you help then I can come and have a drink too!"

They hustled around the kitchen. When everything was done, Robin finally got herself, the bowl of Cioppino she was waiting all night to try and took it to the table. Everyone ate and enjoyed their meals and Robin was surprised at the flavor of the Cioppino. It was delicious. They all laughed and talked until four-thirty in the morning, then they all got up to leave at the same time.

"Robin can I catch a ride home with you again?" Lee asked with a grin on his face, after having consumed far too much alcohol.

"Of course. Come on let's go. Goodnight everyone. See you Wednesday Jose. Can you get home alright Jose, do you need a ride?"

"Yes Robin I have already called a taxi. Maria left hours ago as usual. See you next week. You two have fun." He punched Lee on the shoulder and winked at Robin.

They started driving and Lee asked if they could go to her place. Of course she said yes. They were there in no time sitting on her couch.

"Do you want some coffee or something to drink or eat?"

"No thanks. I just want to kiss you again, and again, and again." His voice trailed off as he covered her lips with his. They were just as passionate as before and Robin felt herself go numb. They were entwined in each other's arms kissing and his one hand was feeling for her breast as the other rubbed her back. Robin's arms were wrapped around Lee's back as her hands ran up and down his back, into his hair and down his back again.

"Can we go somewhere more comfortable?" Lee asked

"Why Mr. Cotton, you are awfully forward with your women." Robin replied in a southern drawl.

"Yeah. I know. So can we go to your bedroom?"

"Well my goodness, I suppose." Robin responded in the same drawl looking into Lee's eyes.

"Are you sure. I know I'm rushing you but after what I saw last night I can't wait any more. This was the longest day of my life. All I could think about was how beautiful you looked standing here last night in that pink nightgown thing you had on. It's been torture sitting here with you in that outfit," He pointed to her work uniform, "knowing what I saw you in last night."

"When you put it like that, all a girl can say is," she stood up and took Lee's hand and said, "come with me." As she headed for the bedroom. Pausing outside the door they kissed again. Lee held her face gently with both of his hands, his thumbs slowly caressing her cheeks as they continued the kiss. He then picked her up and carried her to the bed, still slowly kissing. Gently he put her down and tried undoing the buttons of her top. They were not easy to undo, so Robin got up and said "I'll be right back."

She went and locked the front door, turned off the lights, went to the bathroom and freshened up, brushed her teeth, put on some perfume and the pretty pink nightgown from last night. Lee watched her walk across the room to turn out the light and was aroused with what he saw. She then walked towards the bed he was laying in, his clothes piled in a heap on the floor. She climbed in beside him.

"You are so beautiful." He said as he slipped the nightgown over her head and kissed her when he was done. "Do we need any kind of birth control here or are you on the pill?"

"I'm not on the pill. I haven't needed to be for months. So we will need something. Do you have anything?"

"Yeah. I think I've got something in my wallet." He started to get up.

"Never mind. I have some right here." She leaned over and opened her night table drawer.

"A woman who's prepared for anything. I love it." He laughed.

"I just bought them today silly. I hoped we would be in this position tonight."

"You trashy woman. I think I'm in love." He rolled over and the kissing began again. But it didn't stop there. They made love with a passion Robin had never known before. He was gentle and yet so powerful. Robin had lost all of her senses and all track of time and place. She was somewhere else and nothing in the world mattered while they made love. It seemed to last forever.

When they awoke and it was almost noon. Lee got up to go to the bathroom then climbed back in bed. They made love again. Lee took Robin back to that place she had been to for the first time ever, last night. It was sheer pleasure again. They nodded off to sleep wrapped in each other's arms.

It was ten to three when they woke up. They got up this time and Robin prepared omelets, toast and coffee for them. Lee sat at the kitchen table and watched her. They never did make it to the beach that day.

Chapter Thirteen

"Robin are you okay?" Lee asked as he put one arm around her shoulder and tried to drive with the other hand. Robin was in tears and couldn't talk, she just nodded her head.

"Did he hurt you or something? Are you sure you're okay?" Robin was laughing between her tears.

"Just keep going until I say stop." She managed to get out. They continued driving toward the airport.

"What time is it?" Robin asked as she wiped her eyes then blew her nose.

"About six-fifteen. Why?"

"Could you please stop at the next hotel."

"Are you nuts? What for? Are you sure you're okay? What did that guy do to you?"

"I'll explain in a minute. Let me pull myself together first and just stop so I can freshen up. Please."

Lee drove until he came to the 'Airport Inn'.

"Is this alright? Do you want to use the washroom or something?"

"No I don't want the washroom. Can you go get a room?"

"What do you want a room for?" Lee asked with a puzzled look on his face. Robin leaned over to Lee and wrapped her arms around his neck, kissed him on the lips and said, "Because I want to make love to you right here, right now. That asshole just made me realize how much I love you, and why I love you. All these years I blamed myself for the way he treated me. I could never get over this hang-up I've had about myself and the way I feel, the way I think, how I feel about you and our relationship, and why I'm so insecure. I can't really explain it to you, but right now I need to feel your arms and your body close to me and for you just to make love to me."

"Wow. I'll be right back." Lee jumped out of the car and ran into the hotel. Robin went and got her make-up bag and a clean T-shirt and underwear out of the trunk. Lee came back out with a key and off they went to the room. He opened the door and stood aside to let Robin in. As she walked by she grabbed Lee's hand and pulled him along to the bed with her. The door closed behind them. They had their clothes off in no time and were making love with a different passion than ever before. Lee could feel Robin's desire and her need to be loved. He could feel a passion in her kiss that had never been this strong before. When they were finished they lay embraced in each other's arms.

"What did he say that brought all this on Rob?" Lee asked as he brushed Robin's hair from her face and kissed her forehead.

"He called me a snotty bitch basically. And said he could now tell everyone that he 'fucked' country star 'Lee Cotton's' wife. Lee sat up.

"I wanna kill the bastard."

"Don't waste your time thinking like that Lee. Besides, I told him that if he knew how to fuck maybe he wouldn't have been married so many times." Lee laughed.

"Good for you Robin. I didn't know you felt so uncomfortable all this time though. Why haven't you ever talked to me about this before?"

"I guess I didn't realize it myself. I knew that I always felt nervous with other men after Don. I always wondered what I did that was so wrong and if it would happen again. Of course when it did, I felt so bad again. And I've still wondered what I did that was wrong."

"Wait a minute here. This goes beyond you and Don, that was twenty years ago. When I had my little slip and did what I did, it brought all the same insecure feelings back you had then, right?"

"Right."

"Robin, we've discussed this over and over. I know what I did to you was so totally wrong. And I've told you over and over that I would take it all back if I could. It was nothing, she meant nothing to me. You've got to remember that. That was like, five years ago. We were just starting to become famous. There were women everywhere and we had been on the road for months. Do you know what it feels like to have beautiful women throwing themselves at you every night and not being able to touch them and being horny as hell cause it's been weeks since you've had sex? Of course you don't and that's no excuse. I know. And I'll never forgive myself for doing that to you, but don't ever blame yourself for that or what he did to you. It was me. It was my fault and my male needs that got in the way. For God's sake Robin, you are the most beautiful woman in the world and I love you more than anything else I will ever have in my life. I've loved you since that first night I met you in Jose's restaurant. Remember those days? You have no reason to feel any insecurities and I'm sorry that I ever had any part in making you feel that way." Lee was shaking and on the verge of tears.

"Lee," Robin sat up beside him and hugged him tight. "I don't care anymore. I realized tonight that he was the one that was wrong. And all of a sudden it all came clear to me that you were too. And it wasn't my fault and if all I can give you is as much love as I can and hope that it will be enough and if it's not..........it's just not my fault!"

"Robin I had no idea you thought it was your fault. How

could you even think that? I'm so sorry. I'm gonna be sorry for that for the rest of my life."

"I don't want you to be sorry anymore Lee. It's the past and it's over. It just took me this long to see the light and now I know I can feel comfortable with you gone for the next three months. For that matter, I think I will feel fine anytime you go on the road from now on. I won't feel that I have to be with you all the time just to make sure you behave. I will miss you so much and I've been so worried about you being gone that long. You better behave mister cause you won't get a second chance again." She laughed and pulled away from Lee. He couldn't look her in the eye. He turned away. Robin put her hands on his face and turned him towards her. Lee was crying.

"Sweetheart, I didn't ever mean to hurt you so bad. All I can say is I'm so sorry. I don't want you to ever hurt again." He wrapped his arms around her and rocked.

"Will you stop saying your sorry. I know you are. And I'm not going to hurt like that ever again. Lee you have no idea how good I feel. I feel free and alive and in love. Wanna go another round?" Now they were both laughing and kissing and starting the fire all over again.

When they were done they had a shower together, got dressed and left the hotel holding hands. They drove to the airport, returned the rental car and checked in for their flight. Everything was on time so they grabbed a coffee from the vending machine and sat down to wait. They were both in baseball caps and sunglasses and they looked very much like celebrities. People starred, but could not figure out who they were. This was the part Robin loved. She loved to be in a crowd and look famous, but the people didn't have a clue who she was. She smiled. Inside she felt so good. She was actually looking forward to be going home now. They were catching a regular flight to Vancouver, the rest of the band would have a private charter waiting for them to arrive and they would all be heading home together.

Finally it was time to board. They checked their luggage, one suitcase and two carry-ons and boarded the plane. Robin sat down beside the window and when the flight took off she blew a kiss and said

"Good bye Victoria!"

They arrived in Vancouver about 20 minutes later. Grabbed the suitcases and found the charter. Everyone else was on board waiting for Lee and Robin. There were hugs and kisses all around. This was where they belonged now, this was their family. Robin relaxed and felt great. Finally, they were going home. After they had taken off and were underway, out came the Tequila. Everyone was talking about what they had done for the weekend. They all had gone in different directions and everyone had a story to tell. Robin had one shot and it tasted so good she felt herself relaxing. Lee looked over at her and gave her that smile. She couldn't control herself. She walked over to where he was standing and put her arms around him and kissed him. Everyone stopped talking and stared at them.

"I can't wait to get home." She yelled. Then held out her glass for another shot. They all filled up their glasses and cheered to Texas and shot them back.

Robin was so tired. She excused herself and went and sat down at the back of the plane. She closed her eyes and knew she could fall asleep so she stood back up and grabbed a pillow and a blanket, made herself comfortable and was gone. She woke up to Lee rubbing her arm saying "Robin we're home Honey, wake up, let's go." She yawned and stretched her arms.

"Home already?" Did I sleep the whole way?"

"Yes you did Mrs. Cotton, lets go, I can't wait to get to the house."

Robin still felt tired and had a horrible taste in her mouth.

"I need to go to the bathroom first and brush my teeth." She grabbed her bag and headed for the bathroom feeling still not quite awake. When she was done they got into the limo that was waiting for them. It was early morning and really warm.

Having come from cool fall weather to warm fall weather. It felt good. Robin asked to have the window open. She hoped it might make her feel more awake. The other guys all lived close to town. Lee and Robin were the furthest away. So two by two they got dropped off and Robin thanked them all again for coming. The guys all shook hands and said they would get together for practice tomorrow and get things ready for the road. Lee and Robin snuggled together in the back of the limo and enjoyed the drive home in quiet.

When they pulled into the driveway Robin felt a feeling of pride warm her heart. It had never felt so good to be home. She loved this house. They had designed it together, it had everything and more than they would ever need.

Chapter Fourteen

Lee spent that Sunday night at Robins. They made love again and in the morning Robin had to get up to go to school. Lee got up with her and they had breakfast together. Then he walked her to school, and she had a hard time leaving. He wouldn't stop kissing her. She giggled all the way to her first class and had a hard time concentrating in the rest of her classes. Lee was going to practice with the guys and would pick her up later for dinner. From then on, they pretty much spent most of their free time together hanging out. They did finally make it to the beach and went as often as they could.

By Christmas they confirmed that they lived together as Lee spent every night he was in town at Robins. Robin didn't go home for Christmas that year, she spent it with Lee's family. They all loved Robin and hoped that finally Lee would settle down and get a normal job, get married and stop living this wild life he had. They didn't understand how he could quit school to play music. Robin couldn't tell them that she loved his music and wanted him to pursue it further and to really get serious about it. However, Robin and Lee talked about it all the time. Robin knew he would make it one day. He had the passion, the desire and the drive. It was in his soul.

After Christmas that year Lee moved all his stuff to Robin's place and it was official. They felt it was the right thing to do as the band was doing really well and they were on the road now for weeks at a time. Whenever Lee was home, he was at Robin's anyway, so why pay double the rent? During the time Lee was away, Robin studied very hard and continued to work at the restaurant. Jose was thrilled that Lee and Robin's relationship had developed as far as it had, but he wanted them to get married. Every time Lee came into the restaurant, Jose would tell him he had to make an honest woman out of her and it wasn't right that they should just live together. Lee would always laugh it off, but that spring...........

It was a beautiful sunny Sunday. Lee asked Robin to pack a picnic and said they were going for a drive. It was going to be Robin's twenty-second birthday on the following Wednesday and the band was going to be out of town and Robin would be at work. He had to do it this weekend. They drove to their favorite spot at the beach and found a place to sit and eat. Robin had made submarine sandwiches, packed a six pack of beer, some chips, cookies, and a couple of apples.

"Robin, you make the best sandwiches! These are really good." Lee complimented as he took a swig of beer and continued eating.

"Thanks. I thought you might like them." Robin also took a swig of her beer. When they were finished eating they lay in the warmth of the sun and napped.

"Come on let's go for a walk." Lee pulled at Robin's hand.

"No, I just want to lay here and enjoy the sun, its so warm and I'm comfortable."

"Come on, come on lazy bones let's just walk down the beach a bit then we can come back and make out." He started tickling and kissing her.

"Oh Mr. Cotton, you do have a way of persuading a girl don't you?"

They went for a walk down the beach holding hands. Robin was barefoot and was enjoying the feeling of the warm sand on her feet. When they had been walking for quite awhile Lee turned to Robin.

"Let's sit down here on the sand." He helped Robin down, but he stayed kneeling. He put one hand in his pocket, checking for the ring box. He then turned and put both hands on Robin's face and kissed her very softly on the lips. He then got up onto one knee.

"Robin, I love you so much and I was wondering if you would consider being my wife?" He then pulled the ring box from his pocket and opened it, took the tiny diamond ring and put it on her finger. She laughed, she cried, she jumped up and hugged him and they rolled in the sand as she was saying, "Yes! Yes! Yes! Oh Lee I had no idea you wanted to get married yet." She wiped tears of joy away.

"Well I don't want to get married right away. But soon. Maybe in a year or so. I just wanted you to know that I am serious about you and that I really do love you. I'm going to be away on your birthday so I hoped this would let you know that even though I'm not here I do love you and I am always thinking about you."

Robin leaned over and hugged Lee and kissed him passionately.

"I'm sorry the diamond is so small, it's all I can afford right now. But I promise you Robin, one day we will never have to worry about how much things cost and then I will get you the biggest diamond ring we can find."

"Lee it's beautiful and I don't care if we never have any money as long as we stay in love, that's all I want. I don't want the way we feel about each other right now to ever go away. So don't worry about diamonds, just worry about how you're going to keep me happy!" They both laughed, got up and started walking, arm in arm, back up the beach to where they had left their things.

Robin could now tell her parents that Lee had moved in. She didn't want to alarm them up to this point. But now that they were engaged she thought it would be okay. They however, were quite concerned and decided to come to Texas to meet this fellow who was going to be their son-in-law. Lee's parents and family were thrilled at the announcement. They said they would like to throw a little party for Lee and Robin. Robin asked if they could wait until her family came so they could all meet each other.

They did all meet and Robin's parents got along great with Lee and his family. Robin was worried that her parents would not fit in with Lee's parents and their friends. Her Mom and Dad were more laid back, easy going, almost hippie type vegetarians. Whereas Lee's family were high in the Houston social circle and belonged to an exclusive Country Club and were much more sophisticated. But it all turned out well. Much better than Robin had hoped.

The main question of the evening of course was, "So, when are you getting married?"

"Soon." Was the best answer they could come up with. Robin wanted to finish school and Lee was away so much right now. So for now it seemed 'soon' would be quite awhile away.

It turned out 'soon' was two more years. Robin had worked very hard at school and was about to graduate. She was now twenty-four years old. And for Lee the past two years had gone very well. The band was now opening for bigger names and they were not doing much of the bar circuit anymore. It meant they were away a lot more now. But things were improving and they were making more money. Robin's graduation ceremony would be in May and her parents and brother would be coming for that. So they decided to have the wedding at the same time in order to save everyone another trip. Lee and Robin decided that since they met at The Sunset Café, that was where they wanted to get married. Lee's parents did not like this idea at all. They had hoped for a big church wedding with a catered reception at the Country Club they belonged to.

Lee and Robin had to sit down with them and explain that this was their wedding and this was the way they wanted it. They explained, that really they had been living together for over two years and this was just a formality to them, not a big extravaganza. They had to convince Lee's mom that it would be done with elegance and in good taste, just not the way she had dreamed it would be. So the arrangements were all made. Graduation one weekend and a wedding the next.

Robin picked out a long, white Spanish looking dress with lots of lace around the bottom, sleeveless, with a sweetheart neckline. She had her hair done up in soft loose romantic curls. She wore a short white veil and her bouquet was pink roses, pink orchids and baby's breath.

Lee wore a black suit with a pink cummerbund and pink roses in his lapel, and his favorite black cowboy boots.

Bo was the best man and his girlfriend Ashley, who had become Robin's closest friend, was the maid of honor. She wore a dress similar in style to Robins, but not as elegant, and in a soft shade of pink. Lee's two brothers, and Robin's one, were all ushers. There were about seventy-five guests. Mostly Lee's family and Lee and Robin's friends that lived in Texas. Robin had decided against inviting her friends from Victoria. Not that she didn't want them to come, she knew it would cost them a lot of money. So instead she sent them announcements that they had been married.

Jose and Maria had rearranged the restaurant just for the wedding. In the center was a circular tiled floor that was usually covered with tables. They had moved all the tables away and arranged the plants around the circle. Above was a huge skylight. The guests were staggered all around on all the different levels of the restaurant. Robin's father walked her through the front doors and down the center "aisle". When the preacher asked who gives this woman, Robin leaned over and gave her dad a kiss and he returned it with a huge hug. The ceremony was very beautiful and lovely soft music was playing in the background. Jose and Maria were crying. Robin cried, her mother cried, Lee's mother cried. But they were all tears of happiness. After the ceremony pictures were taken with almost everyone who was in attendance. Then everyone sat down to a huge feast. All the legal aged guests were given a shot of tequila for the toast to the bride. Jose's idea. Then Jose made the toast to the bride, as a special request by Robin.

"Attention everyone. As a special toast to the bride, I have filled your glasses with tequila, Robin's favorite drink. We quite often have too much of this when we are working. Some times it's the only way we can make it through the night." He chuckled as Maria slapped his arm.

He continued. "Robin has become like a daughter to Maria and myself. We both love her and Lee very much and if you ask them, they will tell you that I told Robin the first time she met my friend Lee, that they would get married and have lots of babies." He looked at Robin and smiled. "You remember Robin? Oh she got so mad at me! See you should listen, I know." He patted his chest. Robin laughed. "Anyway, I would like to wish this happy couple much happiness and a life together filled with much love and lots of babies. Salute! To the bride!" Robin downed that tequila and many more before the night was over. Everyone ate, drank and had a good time. Just before the dancing was to begin Lee took his guitar and went and sat in front of the microphone.

"Robin this is for you." He sang:

"Tonight I leave the world of being alone, and forever to come I will have a love of my own.

Your love has opened not only my eyes, but also my heart.

Never before and never again will a love come to me as beautiful and sweet as you.

I will love you with the love and desire that you deserve and promise to let you become the woman that you need to be.

I hope that you will continue to love me forever. And although we will have bumps and sometimes, potholes along the way, I need you, I love you, I want you to know, I will be here for you from today till forever no matter which road I go down you are always with me in my heart."

They're weren't too many dry eyes in the house. But before long the music was playing and everyone danced. Finally the night was over and it was time for Lee and Robin to leave. Hugs were given all around and Robin told her family she would see them the next day.

Lee's parents had paid for a Honeymoon suite for them at the Four Seasons Hotel in Houston. A white limo drove them to the hotel. They got out and kissed all the way up in the elevator. When they got to their room, Lee picked Robin up and carried her over the threshold.

"Welcome to the start of a new life Mrs. Cotton." They peeled each others clothes off and made love right there on the floor.

Chapter Fifteen

The next two years, Robin continued to work at "The Sunset Café." She enjoyed it and Jose and Maria were more like family to her than her bosses. They took more and more time off now and Robin took over. She planned all of the menus and did all the buying and she now had a helper to do all the prep work.

Robin and Lee had moved into a bigger house, they still rented, but Lee continued with the band, which was doing very well. He was home every three weeks. They had gone Country. They decided this was their sound and was what they most wanted to play. Bo and Ashley were married so were John and Sue. The girls stuck together, and spent weekends and free time keeping each other from getting lonely when the band was on the road. They would shop or go out for dinner, to a movie or bowling. Life was pretty good. When the girls could get away from their own jobs, they would meet up with the guys for a couple of days. One particular weekend the band was opening in Nashville for Alabama, who had consecutively had a number one country song on the charts for the past eighteen months. The girls all wanted to meet the lead singer – Randy Owens. So they flew out for the weekend. They got to meet everyone from Alabama. After the concert they all went for dinner and drinks. While they were all visiting, and enjoying the food and the company, the producer of Alabama's latest album came and introduced himself to Lee and asked if he could meet with him the next day. The next day "Rocket Fuel" was signing themselves to their first major record label.

The next few years went by fast and "Rocket Fuel" became very well known in the country music circle. Country music was getting more and more popular and the band was still opening for other bands, but they were now included in the lineup, not the opening act. They had released a couple of CD's with songs that were getting more and more air -play on the radio. All of a sudden it seemed, country music took off. It changed its sound and was now more rock and blues. "Rocket Fuel" went back to more of their original roots and were soaring to the top with a host of other newcomers to the country music scene. This was so overwhelming to everyone. It happened so fast. The money was all of a sudden pouring in. The records were selling gold in a matter of weeks and platinum in months. And the fame and recognition was instant, or so it would seem to an outsider. Not knowing how many years of struggling these guys had spent and still managed to stay together. Not many bands in the music business got this far with the original band members still together. All of the guys managed to find themselves with offers beyond their wildest dreams. Billy and Joe, who were still not married, enjoyed this and made the most of it, going through women like crazy. The other guys got caught up in the thrill of it all as well. John was pretty stable, he adored Sue and nothing would make him unfaithful. Bo and Lee however, got themselves into a bit of trouble.

Chapter Sixteen

When Robin got out of the limo she just stood and looked at their house and the gardens for awhile.

"God its great to be home!" She said with a tired smile on her face.

Lee grabbed her hand and they went for a walk around the house.

"Wow it sure is. I can't wait to get in the tub and soak for about half a day." Lee said as he put his arm around Robin's shoulders and snuggled into her hair.

"I can't wait to go for a ride on Ginger. I hope she still remembers who I am." Robin's palomino was her favorite horse on the ranch. "It seems like we've been gone forever. Why does it never feel like this when we come home from being on the road?"

"I guess it was just a different kind of trip, it wasn't all work and we actually got to enjoy ourselves quite a bit and relax. Maybe we relaxed too much and it seems like so long since we've had to do any work. I don't know. I'm not going to be here long enough to figure it out before I'm off again."

"Oh, please don't remind me. I'm going to miss you so much!

" Robin snuggled a little closer. Then she pulled away and put her hand over her forehead.

"Three whole months, whatever am I going to do with myself?" She started giggling.

"Well I don't know what you will be doing for three months, but I know what you will be doing for the next two days." Lee grabbed Robin's hands and pulled her to him and kissed her passionately.

"Come on, let's go in and see what mail and messages we have waiting for us. Then we can grab a nap and start to get ready for the next adventure!"

Arm in arm, they walked back to the driveway to pick up their luggage and headed into the house.

Robin called her Mom and Dad to let them know they were home and to fill them in on the details of their trip and tell them all about Victoria and how much it had changed. Her Mom decided they would prepare dinner and bring it over so Robin didn't have to worry about that for tonight. Then she called Lee's family with the same information. Lee's father said he had to talk with Lee about some of the affairs of the ranch and he would be over after dinner for coffee and dessert. Then she settled in sorting out the stack of mail. She could never believe how much mail could accumulate in two weeks. There were the usual bills and junk mail, a letter from Sterling Parker, their lawyer, a couple of Christmas catalogues, all kinds of mail for the bar, some business mail for the band, confirming dates and hotels and such. Robin looked it all over quickly, and then pulled out the stuff for Lee and put the rest aside and made a mental note to go through it after Lee left. It would fill in at least one day with returning correspondence and paying the bills and looking for Christmas gifts.

"Oh shit, Christmas. I can't even think that far ahead yet. Why on earth do they send these out so damn early?" She thought as she stacked the Christmas catalogues on top of the mail pile and went upstairs to put it all in the office, then went to unpack her bag. Lee was already getting his things unpacked and making a new pile of things he would need to take with him and a pile for the laundry and the dry cleaners.

"We will have to go into town tomorrow so I can have this dry cleaning done before I have to leave." Lee stated as he continued to unpack.

"I called my parents and they are going to bring dinner over tonight for us and your Dad wants to talk to you about the ranch so he said he will stop over for dessert and coffee." Robin was going through her bags now adding to the laundry pile Lee had already started.

"Anything interesting in the mail?" Lee asked.

"Oh the usual. I put it all in the office, there's quite a pile for the band and the bar. You'd better make sure you go through it before you leave. Have you checked the answering machine?"

"No, not yet. I don't feel like returning any calls right now. I'll do it after dinner. I want to get my clothes organized and go and check on the animals. Do you feel like going for a ride later?"

"A ride on what?" Robin asked laughing, "bike, horse, Harley?"

"I bet Ginger would be upset if she heard you ask that question! On the horses silly, you said you couldn't wait to go for a ride, so let's go."

"Lee I'm really tired right now and I could sure use a nap. How about we unpack and I get the laundry started, take a nap and then we go for a ride?"

"Sure, sounds great. Actually, I think I could use a nap too. You know you never realize how tired you really are until you stop moving. I think I'm getting old!"

"Don't be silly, you'll never get old!" Robin said mockingly. Lee walked past and smacked her gently on her butt.

"I think I'll grab a quick shower before I start the laundry." She peeled off the clothes she was wearing and entered the ensuite shower in their bedroom. When she got out she gathered up all the clothes and headed for the laundry room to get it started. By the time she got the first load in and headed back to the bedroom, Lee was fast asleep in their bed. Robin climbed in beside him and she was asleep instantly too.

They were awakened by the sound of the doorbell ringing. Robin jumped up and almost fell over she was so dizzy. She regained composure and fully woke up and went to the door. It was her parents with dinner. The door was locked and they hadn't brought their key. They excused themselves for interrupting, but it was five-thirty.

"Sorry Mom and Dad," Robin exclaimed as she hugged them both, "we both fell asleep as soon as we got home. I can't believe we slept this long. Here put dinner in the oven and I'll go get dressed and get Lee. Help yourselves to something to drink."

Robin put the dinner in the oven to keep warm and went to dress. She passed Lee as he was going down the stairs. He had dressed and was going to say Hi.

Robin's Mom had prepared vegetarian lasagna, green salad, and brought frozen mashed raspberries and ice cream for dessert.

"Mom thanks for doing this. It's so great to come home to a home cooked meal. It was delicious." Robin got up to clear the table and put on the kettle for tea and coffee. They talked and laughed and heard all about what each other had been up to since they had left town. Then Lee's parents arrived and they all had dessert, tea and coffee. The women excused themselves and went to the family room and left the guys to talk in the kitchen.

"Honey are you feeling ok?" Robin's Mom asked when they had all sat down.

"Yes, I'm really tired. I didn't realize how much though until we got home. This trip was fun and we all had a fabulous time, but I also found it very draining. First of all I was really nervous about being the M.C. and all, but it was fine. It was fun for me to be in the spotlight for a change. Then seeing people I hadn't seen for a long time was pretty interesting. And Mom, remember

Don Land, the guy who dumped me just before graduation?" her Mom nodded, "well, we had quite the conversation."

Robin proceeded to tell her Mother and her Mother-in-law the gist of the story and how she had been feeling all these years without mentioning exactly what had happened between her and Lee. She didn't think either Mother would be interested in all the details of that story!

While the men were in the kitchen Lee got updated on all the details of the ranch and what crops had to be brought in soon and which animals were okay and which needed attention. When everyone had left, Robin finished up the laundry and Lee started going through the mail. They were both wide-awake now and knew they wouldn't be able to sleep.

"Let's go for that ride now." Lee said when Robin walked past as he sat at his desk.

"Are you nuts? It's too late to take the horses out now!" Robin yelled back as she continued down the hall to the bedroom to put away clothes. Lee put down the mail he was reading, got up from the desk, turned out the light and followed Robin into the bedroom.

"Not on the horses, let's take the Harley and head over to the Honkey-Tonk and see what's shakin. It's only ten-thirty. We can be home by midnight, besides it's a beautiful night. Then we can come home and just the two of us soak in that big ol' tub of ours without having to be in a hurry to get somewhere or go to meet with someone. What'cha say?"

"Well when you put it that way, how could a girl possibly say no. Let me just go freshen up."

Chapter Seventeen

The guys were on the road a lot now. It was great for their careers, but not so great for a relationship. They were going away for months at a time, with only a couple of days off in between gigs. Bo and Lee were the "pretty boys" of the group. They always got the women's attention wherever they went. It was fun and they played right into it. They enjoyed all the attention and adoration. They kept themselves very professional most of the time, playing with women's minds and making them feel like they were giving them their undivided attention. They would connect with someone in the audience and play to them all night. It was fun for them at the end of the night when they would go back to the hotel room they would talk about who they had connected with that night. Occasionally a fan would take it too personal and try to get closer than they should, but the guys usually talked their way out of any preconceived commitments or obligations. However, one trip the band had been away for two months already and still had one more month to go before they could go home. They had gained quite a following and were touring through Louisiana, Arkansas, and finally Oklahoma. They had finished a two-night tour in Tulsa and continued on to Oklahoma City for three shows opening for Marty Stuart. This was a fun tour. Marty was a blast to work with and they all partied a lot.

Lee had connected with a girl in the audience in Tulsa. She was beyond beautiful and he was more than just playing with or to her. He felt something with this woman that he had never felt before. It was like he had known her for a long time, she felt comfortable to talk to and they just had an instant compatibility. She had a great smile, a great figure, and a very outgoing personality. They met after the show and Lee learned her name was Jennifer. They talked most of the night in between beer and a few joints. When the sun had started coming up they said goodbye. Lee gave her a hug and wished it could have been more. But he remembered he had a beautiful wife only a few hundred miles away.

Jennifer showed up for the first concert in Oklahoma City. They connected again and Lee just couldn't resist this time. He met her for drinks after the show and they ended up in Jennifer's hotel room. They had sex. It was good. Lee felt both bad and good. He felt bad that he had betrayed Robin, but it had been too long and he just couldn't take all these beautiful women any more without indulging a bit.

Jennifer showed up again, two nights later for the second show. They met again and Lee figured he had already been unfaithful, why not enjoy it again. He would soon be home. So they spent the night and most of the next day together. Lee told Jennifer that he was very happily married and there was not going to be anything more than sex happening between them. She said she was fine with whatever part of him he was willing to give. When she showed up at the third show, Lee made a point of avoiding making eye contact with her and when they had finished for the night he and the other guys quickly left the party room and headed out to find some food and try to relax inconspicuously.

Bo got himself into a similar situation. Her name was Sasha

and she was a stunning redhead with a body that matched. Her proportions were as awesome as her hair was red! Bo just had to play with this one. He actually was gone for the eight days they were in town. He would show up for the gig and be gone as soon as it was done. He didn't even stick around to do the schmoozing with the V.I.P's who managed to wrangle their way into the party room. On the night of the last concert he had told Lee between songs that he had to get out of there quickly tonight with the guys, or he may not be going home.

Of course, these stories were the highlights on the bus home, and all sorts of jokes were made about the women and the way the guys performed both on and off the stage, and just wait till the wives find out about this. Suddenly Lee panicked, how could he have done this to Robin? All these years together he had never been unfaithful, why this time, what on earth had he done? They all made a pact that this would be between them and it would go no further. But Lee still felt awful. He knew he was going to have to tell Robin himself. He knew that if this got out and someone else told her it would kill her. He loved her so much, he didn't ever want to hurt her. But he already had-she just didn't know it yet.

Chapter Eighteen

Robin went and changed into a pair of black jeans and a new white T-shirt. She rolled up the sleeves and put on a black leather vest that laced up the sides and pulled on her black and white snakeskin cowboy boots. She grabbed her black leather jacket and went back into the kitchen where Lee was already waiting for her. Together they walked out to the garage and Lee made his way to the red Harley. They had a fine choice of other vehicles but this was by far Lee's favorite. They had a white Explorer that Lee drove most of the time. Robin had a white Porsche convertible. Lee also still had his old 1969 Ford pickup that he had when he and Robin first met. But it was now just used around the ranch.

Lee fired up the Harley. The noise rattled the windows in the garage and cut the silence of the clear night air. They both pulled on helmets and headed to the Honkey-Tonk. Robin leaned back and enjoyed the feeling of freedom. She remembered the times when she was terrified to ride the bike with Lee and how over the years she has come to really enjoy the feeling of the fresh air in her hair and on her face. She also liked the feeling of being this close to her husband. As she thought that thought she wrapped her arms around him and gave a big squeeze. He revved the engine and patted her hand. A few miles later they were at the Cotton's Honkey-Tonk Bar and Grille. It was such a rush walking into the place. A country band was playing a Little Texas song, "God Blessed Texas" and most of the crowd were up dancing. They walked over to the bar and took a seat. Robin ordered a beer and Lee ordered a coke. Chet, the bartender, came and brought them their drinks.

"Welcome home Boss." He exclaimed as he shook Lee's hand and came over to Robin and gave her a hug. He pulled up a seat and joined them.

"Hey Chet, what's been happening since we've been gone?" Lee asked.

"Oh the usual. Same old crowd. Same old shit, different day!" He laughed as he said the usual line he gave Lee every time they spoke.

"You know, one day it would be nice to hear something different come out of your mouth. Who is the band they sound pretty good?" Lee listened as they sang Jon Michael Montgomery's "Be My Baby Tonight."

"They're a bar band from the same booking company we always use. Sid, the agent, recommended we try them. They've only been doing the circuit for about ten months and they seem to have gained quite a following. We had them here about six months ago. Didn't you see them then?" Chet looked at Robin and then at Lee.

"I think I saw them." Robin answered. "I recognize that cute lead singer. You know I have this thing for lead singers." She smiled as she patted Lee on the back.

"Yeah well you know, I have this thing for beautiful blondes." Lee said as he gave Robin that smile.

"You two are making me sick. Go home and talk like this. Anyway the band brings in the crowds and the women love them. After they were here last we had a lot of requests to get them back. So this was the soonest we could get them, they are really booked."

"Try to keep them on a steady contract with a steady return time if you can, I think these guys are going places. When they break I would like to meet them Chet. Can you order whatever they're drinking and get them to come and sit over here."

"Sure Boss." Chet got up and went behind the bar as the band was singing "Fishing In The Dark."

When the band finished the set, Chet brought them over to meet Lee and Robin. They were thrilled to meet Lee and they were very polite to Robin. The guys were all talking about music, so Robin excused herself and went to the kitchen to see what was going on back there.

This was where she felt most comfortable. She said hello to the staff and checked the fridge and the pantry out of habit. John the chef came along and told her to keep out of his fridge.

"Oh John, old habits you know. How's everything, any problems I need to know about tonight?"

"No not tonight. We have a problem with one of the suppliers, but I'm sure I can handle it in a day or two."

"Well I'm home now for a while, at least until Christmas. I might take off and meet up with the guys." Robin thought about what she had just said. That was an old habit too. She had always hooked up somewhere with Lee if she hadn't gone with him from the beginning of a tour. But not this time she thought. No way. She was determined to stick her ground on this new decision she had made with herself. "Sorry, John, no I won't be going anywhere. I'll be around if there is anything you need to discuss with me. I'll be by more often now. We can talk on a more regular basis. Are you going to make any changes to the menu for fall?"

They continued on with small talk for a few more minutes. Then Robin heard the band start to play again so she went to join Lee. He had moved from where they had been sitting and Chet pointed towards the office. Robin started walking towards the office. As she walked past a table of mostly men, she got whistled and cheered at. She smiled at the men and politely said "Good evening gentlemen" and continued on her way. When she reached the office she found Lee going over the books.

"Everything okay?" she asked.

"Yeah. I just want to do a quick check. You know, just so I still feel a part of this place. Seeing that band out there tonight made me think of all the years I spent playing in places like this. And look where I've ended up. I just want to make sure that if we suddenly dried up tomorrow that this place would always be here for new guys like them. Robin just listen to them, they are really good. I'll bet you anything they will be big before long." Lee paused to listen to the lead singer sing Garth Brooks', "The Dance." Will you listen to that guys voice!"

"Why don't you get them to open for you sometime?" Robin asked as she stood in the doorway to listen.

"That's a great idea, but we need bands that do their own material. But I will keep these guys in mind. Are you ready to go? Everything looks pretty good here." Lee closed the bank books then added, "Will you be coming by from time to time while I'm away?"

"Yes, I'm ready to go and yes I plan to stop by on a more regular basis. What do you need me to do?"

Lee quickly showed Robin the paper work he was interested in and what information he wanted her to keep track of. This was Robin's fun. Her 'job'. Because Lee was on the road so much, Robin more or less got the bar set up and started when they bought the building. It was something for her to do when she was home. What did concern her was Lee's sudden interest in it. He usually just asked if they were in the Red or the Pink. And that was as far as his concern went. The bar was one of many investments they had. Probably the biggest, and because of Robin's training and background, Lee was comfortable with her doing most of the overseeing. They had an excellent manager who took care of everything day to day. And Lee and Robin would usually check in about once a month, just to make sure things were going as well as they could be.

They went and said goodbye to Chet and Robin told him she would stop by next week. Chet shook Lee's hand and wished him well on the tour.

When they walked outside the fresh air hit them both.

"Can we make this a non smoking bar?" Robin asked laughing as she put on her helmet.

"You know that is one of the coolest things about where we are now. We don't have to breathe that shit every night. I don't think I could go back to the bar circuit."

"Don't worry honey. You will never have to." Robin's stomach flipped as she took a deep breath of the fresh air.

The ride home was heavenly. The sky was clear and the stars were so bright. Lee rode slowly and Robin snuggled into his back taking in the smell of him and his hair as it blew in her face. They pulled in the driveway and Lee drove up very slowly trying to keep the noise to a minimum. When they had parked and put away the helmets they slowly walked arm in arm to the house. Robin went into the big ensuite in their bedroom and started to run the tub.

"Do you still want to have a soak Sweetheart?" She yelled out to Lee who had gone downstairs and was looking in the fridge for something to snack on.

"Absolutely Mrs. Cotton." He yelled back at her with a little grin on his face. He found some of Robin's Mom's leftover lasagna and heated it up in the microwave and brought the plate, two forks and a glass of milk to the bathroom.

"Do you think this is how normal people live?" He asked as he put the plate on the edge of the tub, took his clothes off and stepped in.

"What's normal?" Robin asked as she stepped into the tub and settled in front of Lee with her back to his front.

"I don't know. We've never had a normal life have we?" Lee put a fork-full of lasagna in his mouth.

"It's normal to us, just not to anyone else."

"Do you ever wish your life had been normal or different from this one that we have?"

"Sometimes I would like to slow down a bit. And I know that one day it will, but overall I have just as much fun as you do. And I really enjoy being your wife. You make me feel so special when I go anywhere with you. Just that feeling that I'm yours and you're mine. And knowing that you are doing something that you love and we are having this much fun, it kind of doesn't seem fair. But I'm not complaining."

"You never complain about anything."

"That's cause life is good. But if you don't stop shoveling all that food into your mouth without giving me any I'm going to start complaining."

Robin turned to face Lee and he fed her three mouth fulls and then kissed her.

"Thanks." She said and started to turn her back towards him again but he stopped her and leaned over and kissed her again. Robin wrapped her arms around his neck and she played with his shoulder length hair as she kissed him back. A few moments later, Lee stood up, grabbed a towel and dried himself off. He took Robins hand and helped her out of the tub and dried her off. Then he picked her up and carried her to the bed. He went and turned out the lights and snuggled in beside her. And what began with an innocent kiss turned into passion that lasted until they were exhausted. They fell asleep wrapped in each other's arms.

Chapter Nineteen

When the guys arrived home from the tour, Lee was a mess. He knew that what he had done was so very wrong. He tried to convince himself that it was just sex and it had meant nothing to him. He just didn't want to tell Robin and yet he knew he had to.

Robin was at the Sunset Café working when Lee arrived home. He dropped off his stuff and jumped into his truck and headed to the restaurant to see her. He purposely didn't call first, he needed the time to think of how he would explain this all to Robin. He stopped and bought her a dozen pink roses. When he arrived at the restaurant, he was greeted at the door by Maria. He gave her a big hug and she told him that Robin and Jose were in the kitchen. He walked through the restaurant carrying the roses and quietly walked into the kitchen. Robin was preparing some food and Jose was at the sink washing up some dishes. Jose turned first and spotted Lee who quickly made a "sshh" guesture over his mouth. Then he walked up behind Robin and wrapped his arms around her. She jumped and instantly turned to face Lee. Her arms wrapped themselves tightly around him and her lips found his automatically. They kissed for what to Jose seemed like forever! He finally cleared his throat and they separated lips, but still hung on to each other.

"Hi Jose." Lee said without taking his eyes off of Robin. "And hello to you too Sweetheart. God I've missed you."

"I've missed you too. When did you get home?" Robin asked kissing him again.

"Just now. I went home and unloaded and stopped to buy you these," as he pulled the roses from behind her back, "and got here as fast as I could. Do you have to stay or can you leave a little early tonight?" Lee turned toward Jose as he asked that question.

Robin looked at the flowers and then at Lee with a huge smile on her face.

"I was planning to take a couple of days off so we could hang out together for a while, how do you feel about that?"

"I would love it maybe we can go away somewhere quiet and just relax for awhile. How about up to California or Mexico?"

"I was thinking maybe Dallas, someplace a little closer. Are you not tired of travelling?"

"Actually, yes I am. But I thought that maybe it would be nice for you to get away for a change."

"I don't need to go anywhere as long as you're around." Robin wrapped her arms around Lee again and kissed him. "God I've missed you. Let's go home."

Robin left her car at the restaurant and hopped in beside Lee in his truck. They drove the seven miles home talking all the way. Robin had stuff to tell Lee about what had been going on and he had all kinds of tales to tell her, even though they talked almost everyday while he was on the road it was usually a quick "Hi, I'm okay, a little tired, talk to you tomorrow." Type of conversation.

"Lee, you look different, is everything okay?"

"What do you mean I look different?" Lee asked laughing quickly to try and ease some of the tension that he felt.

"I don't know. Just something is different about you."

Oh my God he thought, she can tell. How can women do

this? How do they know? What am I going to tell her? When am I going to tell her? How can I tell her?

"I think its just your hair, it's grown a lot or something." Lee heard Robin saying as he tuned back into her conversation.

"Yeah I guess. I haven't had it cut for a long time. I haven't even showered or washed it today yet. I just ran in the house and dumped my stuff and got over here to see you. I didn't even stop and look around at home, what's new there?"

Robin rambled on about the house and the new neighbors that had moved in at the beginning of the month. How both of their families had been. She was telling him what was new at work when they pulled into the driveway.

Lee knew he had to make love to her right now. Maybe that would make everything all right. He would feel better. So while she was still talking he leaned over and kissed her long and hard. When he pulled away he said

"Can you be quiet for ten minutes so I can catch up on some lost time?"

She giggled and they both jumped out of the truck and ran into the house. They were naked in no time and making love on the kitchen floor. After they had finished they went and had a shower. Robin washed Lee's hair for him and massaged his back.

"Oh that feels so good. You know coming home makes me wish I never had to go away again. Having you here and missing you so much is so hard."

"Yes but," Robin said while she washed and rinsed off her own hair, "you are doing what you love to do and having a good time and its all coming together."

"Yeah, I know. But it's still hard." His mind flashed back to Jennifer and he shuddered.

"Are you cold?"

"No no, just tired and glad to be able to relax. So, speaking of relaxing where shall we go for a couple of days?" Lee turned off the shower and they both dried off and went to their bedroom.

Lee had his towel wrapped around his waist and lay down on the bed.

"My own bed! I almost forgot what it feels like."

"You say that every time you come home! You're the guy who says he can sleep anywhere."

"Well I can. But it's still nice to have a place to come home to and a bed that really just belongs to me that someone else doesn't sleep in every other night!" He looked at Robin with an almost questioning look on his face. With that comment he suddenly thought about her sleeping in that bed every night alone while he was away. Did she have as many needs as he did? What if she found someone else to fulfill them while he was away? It was a long time this time. She was so beautiful. She must get offers all the time. How could I not see this before? How could I let myself be so foolish and not think about her needs? She enjoys sex with me. I wonder if she would do it with someone else just for the sake of having sex and nothing else and not let it mean anything to her?

"What are you staring at?" Robin asked as she was dressing.

"Hmm....Oh, what, what did you say honey? I was just trying to think of where we could go." He lied.

"Would you like to go right now or tomorrow or maybe let's just go out for a nice dinner and stay here tonight. You seem to be enjoying just lying on your own bed! I bet you would probably love to sleep in it?"

"Actually that sounds great. Let's go to some fancy restaurant that we've never been to before, some place that no one will recognize us and just catch up on everything and then come home. I really, really need a good night's sleep."

"Okay. I know just the place. It's new and I've heard great things about it. You know the new mall over on Parkside? it's a new building right next door. I'm not sure what they specialize in, but it is apparently great food. Want to try it?"

"You're the food expert. Whatever you say."

Robin went to the phone and called information to get the

restaurant's number. Then she called to make a reservation for seven p.m.

When she went back to the bedroom to tell Lee, he was fast asleep. She stared at his face for what seemed like forever. He looked so relaxed lying there. But he also looked like a stranger. It always took a while to get used to him every time he came back from being on the road. This time she noticed that too much travelling and probably too many late nights were starting to change his looks. He was still so very handsome. Just looking at him lay there, Robin felt the power of his good looks, but she also saw something a little different. She couldn't quite figure out what it was. Oh well, she thought I will just cuddle in beside him and enjoy the feel of his body back beside me again.

When they woke, they got dressed and went to dinner. Lee was hoping they would have some privacy, but that was impossible now. He had become too big of a star. The staff at the restaurant was very understanding and moved them to a secluded table beside a window overlooking the park. They ordered chateaubriand with braised vegetables, roasted potatoes and a very fine bottle of red wine.

While they were waiting for their food, they talked about everything. Lee decided that it was time they bought their own house.

"Robin, I'm making a ton of money now, I think it's time we settled down in a place of our own and I also think you should quit working at the restaurant."

"How can you even think to ask me to do that? It's the only sanity I have in this life we have between us. When you're away I need something stable and someone to turn to and feel safe with. What do you think I should do all day and night when you're on the road?" Robin was shocked that Lee had even considered her leaving the Sunset Café.

"Slow down honey. I just thought that we don't need the money and maybe you would like to do something else for a change and........."

Robin interrupted, "What do you think I went to school for for all those years? This is what I moved to Texas to do. I don't want to do anything else. I love Jose and Maria. They have done so much for me, for us. I can't imagine working anywhere else. And I can't believe that you don't understand Lee, they were your friends before I knew them and before I knew you."

"Sorry. I just thought that maybe you might like to come on the road with us a bit more and if you didn't have a job then you would be free to join me. And besides I don't really think that my wife needs to work in a restaurant." That last statement sounded a little too conceited for Robin's liking.

"So my job's not good enough for Mr. Lee Cotton, the famous Country Music Star?"

Just then their dinner was brought to the table. While the chef carved the beef, Robin glared at Lee and he could not keep eye contact with her. He took a mouthful of wine and turned to look out the window as he swallowed it. Robin continued to stare at him thinking that perhaps he had become too big for himself! When the chef had finished placing all the food on their plates and filled up their wine glasses, Lee put his hand on top of Robin's and said,

"I'm sorry honey. I should have known better. I know how much you love your job, but I love you. And I really need you to be with me on the road sometimes. Especially when we go away for these long trips, I miss you too much." Oh my God, Lee thought to himself, I can't tell her here. But this is leading right to what I have to say. How do I stop before I say too much. He didn't have to. Robin started talking then.

"I'm sorry too. But what you don't see is that I've had to become quite independent since you're gone so much and I feel very comfortable in my life right now. Don't get me wrong. I miss you terribly when you're gone. And I would love to be with you. But, what am I supposed to do while you set up, then jam for a couple of hours, then go and perform for three or four hours, then go and sweet talk all the groupies for a couple of hours, then go eat and drink and don't go to bed till sunup? Then ruin the next day by sleeping half of it away and then starting all over again. That is your life Lee and I'm not trying to condone it and I know I'm a part of it, but I can't be a part of it like that anymore. I would like to change the subject a bit and say that I would love for us to buy our own house though, that is a great idea. Then we will have a place away from all the crowds and fans so that when you come home, we can just be alone together. Let's eat and talk about this later, this food looks fabulous!"

Lee resisted the urge to continue with the conversation and for a brief moment he actually felt justified in having an affair. It serves her right. If she doesn't want to be a part of my life then this is what is going to happen. I have needs and desires and I can't hold out till I get home. It's too damn hard. I can't stop now. This is my job. This is what I've wanted to do all my life. Does she think I should have stuck to playing the bar circuit so I could be close to home and wouldn't have to travel so much? I thought she understood right from the start that this was where I always knew I would be someday. They ate in silence for a long time. Finally Robin spoke.

"How's your meal?"

"Great, really great." Lee answered and smiled at her knowing very well that he hadn't really tasted a single bite. He took a mouthful of wine and asked how her dinner was.

They finished dinner and ordered a slice of chocolate cheesecake and two Spanish coffees for dessert. The conversation had changed to small talk about the tour and what Lee was going to be doing while he was home.

On the drive home Lee asked, "Do you want to go dancing, or out to a show, or for a drink or something, it's too early to go home."

He knew that he was just trying to prolong the inevitable, but he thought he could at least try to put it off for a little longer.

"I don't know Lee. Do you really think that we can just walk into a bar like we used to? We will be mobbed and people won't leave you alone."

"Does that bother you Robin?"

"Well, yes it does a little. But I know you love it so I will go for you."

"That's not exactly the answer that I was hoping to hear."

"Lee I love you and want to share your life. But lots of times I feel left out and would just rather stay at home."

Lee's tone suddenly changed. Angrily he said while he turned the truck in a U turn in the middle of the road,

"Well darlin', if that's how you feel lets go home because I have something I need to talk to you about."

They rode home in silence. When they got there, Lee jumped out of the truck, slammed the door and went inside the house, not even waiting for Robin. He left the front door open, went to the refrigerator and got a beer. He opened the bottle and threw the cap against the wall. He was leaning against the wall chugging the beer when Robin walked in.

"What the hell's the matter with you?" She asked angrily.

Calmly Lee started to answer,

"You're not going to like what I have to tell you and I've been sick about it for days. But after the conversation we have had tonight I don't feel quite as bad as I did."

Robin stared at him and took in each of his words. She could tell by the way he was speaking that this was very serious. She knew it was about to change her life.

"Robin, I never wanted to ever hurt you. But I..............."
Robin interrupted.

"What was her name?"

"Jennifer."

"Do you love her?"

"No."

"Will you be seeing her again?"

"No."

"Why are you telling me then?"

"Because I can't live with myself."

"Have there been others?"

"No. Never."

"Will there be others?"

"I don't know. That depends on you. After what you have said tonight, I would wager that there will be others because you don't want to leave your job and come on the road with your husband."

"How dare you turn this around and make it my fault. I've been here for you all these years and never once have I needed to be with someone else."

"No you don't need someone else. You've got your job and your new independence. That's all that matters to you. Well I need more. I need you to be with me and support me. You knew this was where we would be one day and it just doesn't seem as important to you as it once did. You helped me through all the tough times. You were my support. You supported me when my parents thought that this was just a dumb dream, you were there from the start through the good and the bad. Having no money to having more than we ever dreamed of. What happened? Why don't you care anymore?"

"Look what good it did me! Being the good wife there to support my husband and look what he does, screw around on me!"

"Robin I'm sorry. I can't say it enough. But you have no idea what it's like out there now. I was away for three months. With no sex and getting offers beyond my wildest dreams every night. Eventually any normal red-blooded guy can't just walk away anymore. I didn't care about her. I just needed to make love to a woman. To be held. And to hold. She knew this, I told her it was nothing more than sex, that was all I could and would give her."

"You self righteous son-of-a-bitch! You better pack your bags and get out. I don't think I can stand to see your face around here." Robin walked into the bathroom and slammed the door. She put the lid down on the toilet, sat down and started to cry.

Chapter Twenty

The next morning Lee and Robin woke to the sounds of chickens cackling and the sun shinning in through their own bedroom window. Robin climbed out of bed first stretching slowly and went to the window and pulled open the blinds.

"Hey, don't, that hurts my eyes." Lee grumbled as he rolled over and covered his head with the blankets.

"Sorry, I forgot YOU usually never get to see this part of a day!" Robin joked.

"Get up sleepy–head we have a lot of stuff to do today. What do you want for breakfast?" Robin went into her huge walk-in closet and came out wearing a floral bathrobe.

"I dunno. Surprise me!" Lee mumbled with his head still under the covers.

As Robin made her way to the kitchen looking through the house with the light of the day, she made a mental note that she really needed to dust! 'Oh well she thought to herself, when Lee leaves I'll have lots of time for housework.'

When she got to the kitchen she opened the fridge. Her Mom had gone shopping for them the day before and picked up a few necessities like milk, eggs, bread, some fruit and fresh vegetables. Robin had enough ingredients to make a couple of omelets and toast. She turned on the coffee and went to work on the omelets.

Lee staggered down from the bedroom, "God woman I need coffee and a local newspaper. I'm usually going to sleep at this time of morning." He glanced at Robin who was giving him the evil eye and threatening him with her egg flipper. "Just kidding sweetheart! So what is the plan of action for today boss?" He asked, quickly changing the subject.

They ate breakfast discussing what had to be done. Dry cleaners, pay bills, pick up some groceries. The band was going to meet at two p.m. to get their equipment organized and get preparations finalized for the tour. Robin and Lee decided they would plan to get as much done as they could by noon then go for lunch and Robin would drop Lee off and he could catch a ride home with someone. They slowly ate breakfast, going through all the bills Robin had pulled out of the mail the previous day. When they were organized, they took the Explorer and headed into the city.

They got everything done that they had hoped to get done and decided to have lunch at the 'Cotton's Honkey Tonk Bar and Grill'.

When they arrived, Chet came right over to tell Lee that he had secured the band from the previous night for a one-week appearance for each of the next six months.

"Good job Chet! Keep up the good work while I'm gone, and don't let my wife get too close to that lead singer!"

Robin looked at Lee with a look that said, "You're dead meat pal!"

Lee stared back without any expression on his face.

Robin wondered if he was serious and where this comment came from. Was he actually concerned about leaving her home alone? 'Hmm' she thought, this is different, usually the shoe's on the other foot. Maybe he is worried about me staying home this time. After all, I've been on tour with them ever since.........

Robin didn't want to go there. That was a long time ago. We both have changed since then and Lee and I have a strong marriage now, stronger than ever. He should have no reason to worry about me unless maybe he thinks I will get back at him or get revenge or something. Wow this is weird. Maybe I'm making too much out of this comment. Maybe I should be wondering if he can be trusted again, or if I should be going with him. No, no stop thinking like this. We are strong and we are in love and we both feel very comfortable with our lives. Why would we do anything to change what we have?

Just then Chet left and Robin tuned back into what Lee was saying. He was asking Robin what she would like for lunch.

"I think I'll have one of John's juicy burgers, 'cause while you're away I'm going to be eating salads and healthy food. So this will be my last indulgence."

"Are you dieting again Robin?"

"No not really. But I know I won't be cooking huge meals just for myself. So I'm planning on making it easy and just hanging out, going riding, working in the yard, doing some work on the house. Getting ready for Christmas. Pam said she and the baby and maybe Marty would come for a visit. I hope they do. We had such a great time at the reunion. I really miss having her around. You know it's really funny, we have kept in touch over the years and it was just like old times seeing her again. It was like our lives were meant to cross and keep in touch. I know we have lots of friends here, but you know there is nothing like an old dear one who knew you back when and who you had secrets with and you can just be yourself with."

"Aren't you yourself with me and our friends?" Lee asked concerned.

"Yes. But I'm a different me with you and them then I was with her and all my friends back home. Living here has changed me. The life we have has changed me, your fame and the money we have has changed the both of us. But she knew me before I was the 'me' I am now, and none of this life," Robin waved her arm through the air, "matters to her or changes our friendship. We are true friends because that is all that matters to us is the friendship. The rest of this stuff she doesn't like me for, just me! Where most of the people we know are in the business or they just want to get close to you for one reason or another. Do you understand what I mean?" Robin reached over and placed her hand on top of Lee's.

"Yeah, I guess, a bit. I guess I don't really have any friends like that because we're all still together and we've all changed together. We've gone through everything with each other and that in itself is pretty amazing, we have managed to stay together not only as a band but also as best friends through it all."

"So you are you with them, but don't you feel like someone else when you are doing business, or performing?"

"I never really thought about it before, but yes, you're right. I do act different when it's just us guys together and then when I'm with other people. Do you think that is what describes true friendship?"

"Absolutely! You must see it. How we are when we are alone and then when we are with other people."

"Yeah. Well then I hope for you, Pam will be able to come and the two of you will be able to visit and have some more fun together." Lee leaned over and kissed Robin on the cheek.

"Let's eat. All this talk has made me hungry."

After they ate lunch, Robin dropped Lee at the warehouse/office the band used to store all their equipment in when they were home. She kissed him goodbye and said she would surprise him with a great home cooked meal when he got home. She stopped off at the supermarket and picked up a baron of beef and a whole bunch of fresh vegetables. She would cook the roast and stir -fry the vegetables and serve it with wild rice. Something decadent for dessert. What should it be? Something fruity or chocolate or maybe chocolatey fruit. That was it. A chocolate fondue with fruit. She went and picked out some fresh strawberries and raspberries, some honeydew melon, and cantaloupe, grapes and pineapple. That would be enough and any leftovers she could use for herself when Lee left. She picked out a very expensive bottle of Bougelais, and some Kaluha and Grand-Marnier to use in the chocolate sauce. As she walked past the floral department, she picked out four bouquets of fresh cut flowers as well as a dozen assorted candles. She also picked up a whole pantry full of other groceries so she wouldn't have to come back into town for a few days after Lee left.

Robin loaded the groceries into the truck and decided to take a walk around the strip mall that was attached to the supermarket. She picked up some stamps and envelopes, a couple of trashy romance novels, a few decorating and cooking magazines. She stocked up on the essentials like toilet paper and deodorant, toothpaste and a new toothbrush for Lee to take with him, some laundry soap and cleaning supplies. Then she went to a couple of clothing stores. She wasn't really looking for anything in particular, but she came across a beautiful soft pink sexy negligee set. It reminded her of the pink nightgown she wore when her and Lee first started dating. He would always ask her to wear it, but it never stayed on for very long. He always said that he thought she looked gorgeous in pink. So on impulse she bought it.

It was four o'clock when she arrived home. She unloaded and put away all of her purchases then put the roast in the oven and was going to start the dessert. When she sat down she realized she was exhausted. So she went and lay down on her bed for a nap.

She woke with a start at six forty. 'Holy cow. I guess I was more tired than I thought. I think maybe we tried to do too much today.' She got up and went and prepared the vegetables and fruit and made the chocolate sauce for the fondue. She set the table and took the flowers from the pail she had placed them in and found lovely vases to arrange them. She placed one bunch on the dining room table, another in the family room, one in the kitchen and one in their bedroom. Then she went to the china cabinet and picked out an assortment of candleholders and placed a set of tapers on the dining table, a variety of tapers, votives and pillars in the family room and some of the nice scented candles in the bedroom. She removed the tags from the negligée and hung it in her closet. She wanted everything to be romantic tonight. She would only have him to herself for one more night after tonight.

Just then the phone rang. Robin hesitated before picking it up, she was going to let the machine get it so she wouldn't have to get into a long conversation with someone she didn't want to talk to tonight. She still wanted to have a bath and freshen up. She picked it up on the fourth ring. It was Lee saying they were having a few beers and he would be home soon. Her heart sank. 'How could they?' she thought to herself. 'All of them have women waiting for them, they will have tons of time together in a couple of days, why do they have to do this tonight?'

"How long will you be?" she asked, trying not to sound disappointed.

As if reading her thoughts he replied,

"Don't worry we all have places we want to be tonight. What time will dinner be ready?"

"In about an hour." She replied cautiously back.

"Ok. I'll be home by then. See you soon."

"Ok. Bye."

As she hung up she stared at the phone, hoping that he would be there in an hour. She went upstairs and turned on the water for her bath. Then went back to the kitchen to check the roast and put the rice on. She went back upstairs and lit one candle and poured some 'Giorgio' scented bubble bath into the tub. She picked out a sexy dress she had worn to an awards show a few months back. It was something that she could never wear in public again. Then she chose a matching lacy bra and panty set and a pair of stay-up nylons. She placed them all on the lounge chair in the dressing room area of the bathroom. She turned out the lights, stripped off her clothes and stepped into the tub. Robin closed her eyes and let the scented water carry her mind off to someplace else. She lay in the tub for about twenty minutes then shaved her legs and underarms, stood up and rinsed herself off with the hand held shower, stepped out and dried off. She sprayed her entire body with 'Giorgio' cologne then dressed in the clothes she had laid out. She found a sexy pair of strappy black high heels that worked well with the orchid colored dress. She applied the simplest of make-up and put her hair into a romantic French roll with loose tendrils hanging all around her face and neck. She was walking to the kitchen as she heard a car coming up the driveway. She looked at the clock it was forty-five minutes since he called. She let out a silent sigh. She didn't want this night to be ruined. She quickly went to the family room and lit the candles turning down the lights as she went to the kitchen.

Just as she got to the kitchen, Lee, Joe and Billy all came in the back door. Robin could see they had had a few. Lee was saying as he was coming in,

"Honey we came back here for a couple........"

Then his eyes caught sight of his wife and he stopped in mid step and in mid sentence. "Oh wow. I don't think it's a good idea for you guys to be here right now."

"Hi Joe, Hi Billy. Come on in. Lee will pay for this later!" Robin smiled innocently.

They both took one look at Robin and said no they had better be getting home as well. And they turned and left, not even saying goodbye to Lee.

"Holy Christ you look hot. What's this all about?" He wrapped his arms around her and kissed her neck. "Oh God you smell so good. Can I talk you into taking a walk upstairs with me?"

Robin could see and feel that he was aroused but she wanted to make this night last longer.

"Not right yet big fella. But if you're good, maybe later. Right now I would like you to open this bottle of wine and then go and have a shower, then dinner will be ready and we will talk about what we can do later."

"Come on I want you right now, right here if I have to." He hugged her again and started kissing her very passionately. Robin wrapped her arms around his shoulders and kissed him back just as passionately as he kissed her. She ran her fingers through the long hair that she loved so much, then she wrapped her leg around his and continued to kiss him. She knew she was driving him crazy and she loved it.

"Go and have a shower please and get changed." Robin gave him one last kiss on the end of his nose, then handed him the corkscrew and bottle of wine.

While he was opening the bottle, he kept looking back at Robin.

"Wow I'm glad we didn't decide to go anywhere else besides here tonight. We have a lot of stuff to still get arranged. Joe's drum kit needs some repairs done to it or some new snares. And we decided we need a new steel guitar. Hopefully we can use the one we have for this tour and get a new one when we get back. I just hope it will make it through the trip. Oh sorry Honey, you probably don't want to hear about my business right now do you?" He poured them each a glass of wine and handed Robin hers.

"Cheers!" They clanked glasses, then kissed.

"Well I guess I'd better go get cleaned up, because by the way you look and smell and the way it looks in this house and the smell of that dinner.........what are we having anyway?"

"Never mind just go get changed." Robin pushed Lee towards the stairs.

While he was in the shower she heated up her sauté pan and quickly stir-fried the vegetables. When they were done she placed them on a platter and put them in the oven with the rice to keep warm. She had set the table with all the 'good stuff', china, crystal, and silverware. They rarely used it and it was so beautiful that tonight Robin felt it was time to start using these things. She felt really good about tonight and Lee's tour. For the first time in years she felt comfortable with her life and felt a peacefulness and confidence and she liked it.

She had taken the roast out of the oven before she started the vegetables so now it was ready to carve. She decided to carve it now and put the slices on a platter instead of carving it at the table like she usually did. She had all the food ready so she lit the candles on the dining room table and put on a Michael Bolton CD. It wasn't country, but it was romantic.

Lee came down the hall dressed in black jeans and a black collar-less dress shirt with the top couple of buttons opened. He had on a black belt with silver conchos all around it. His hair was still wet and Robin could smell that he had used CK-1 cologne.

"This is really nice of you to do Rob."

"Well hopefully I'm going to get something out of it too!" She winked at him. Lee wrapped his arms around her waist and looked into her eyes.

"You know I'm really going to miss you this trip. The past few years you've been on tour with me, and I never really thought much about it. It was just what we did together and it never really crossed my mind, but you look so comfortable and happy to be staying at home this time I kind of feel sad. I think I'm really going to miss you. I hope this is what you really want."

Robin pulled away, and held Lee's hand as she led him to the dining room table.

"Well for the first time in a long time I really am glad to be staying at home. I don't quite know why, or how to explain it, but I just know it's the right thing to do."

"Then if that's ok with you, I will have to be ok with it too."

"Good then let's eat!" Lee pulled out Robin's chair for her and he filled both of their wineglasses and went and sat down. Robin passed the sliced roast to Lee and served herself the vegetables and rice, and then they traded.

"I'm so glad you cooked the vegetables this way, it's going to be a long time before I will get to eat this good again. Will you make sure you have a meal like this ready when I come home?"

"Of course."

They continued with small talk throughout dinner and ate very slowly. They finished off the bottle of wine and really enjoyed each other's company. They didn't leave the table until Michael Bolton and then Celine Dion's CDs had both finished. Robin only put the two in the player, she couldn't find anything else that was 'right' for tonight. When Robin got up to clear away the dishes Lee changed the CDs and loaded up the carousel with his choices.

"Do you want to eat dessert right now or wait awhile?" Robin asked from the kitchen as she stirred the chocolate sauce. Lee came into the kitchen to see what was for dessert.

"I think we should maybe pour a glass of that liqueur and take this dessert to the 'fun room', relax a bit and then eat it."

That's what they did. Robin could feel the effects of the wine so she was happy to just coast a bit. Lee lit the rest of the candles in the family room and turned off the lights. They sat beside each other on one of the floral couches and sipped on the liqueur.

"I'm hoping to do a lot of writing this trip. I think the time apart will be really inspirational for me. I hope I will get a new perspective on being in love and having to be apart from the person you really love. I've already got a couple of tunes in my head, I just need some great lyrics to go with them."

"I know you will come up with something awesome. You seem to always thrive when there is a change in our lives." She looked at him with an almost questioning look on her face.

"Yeah, some of our biggest hits came from when we were apart for those six months. I'm not saying that that was a good thing, it was just really a time full of opportunity for my songwriting."

Robin put her arm around Lee's shoulder and leaned into his ear. She inhaled the scent of him as she spoke.

"You better make sure that's all you'll be doing, writing from your feelings!" She laughed as she ran her hand through his hair and kissed him softly on his lips. She pushed him onto his back and lay on top of him still kissing. As the kiss ended she climbed off, he pulled her back.

"Where do you think you're going?"

"I just want to take off my shoes."

"Oh."

When Robin bent over to undo the clasp on her shoe, she decided right now was a good time to get comfortable, so after she took off her shoes she unzipped her dress and pulled it over her head and sat there in her sexy pink lingerie. Lee became very aroused. He leaned her back onto the couch and kissed her deeply. Without saying a word he looked her in the eyes as he ran his hands over her breasts and down her stomach to the top of her panties, then inside her panties, then out and down her legs, over the stay-up nylons. He didn't let his eyes leave hers once. They could both feel the passion in the room. It was so very intense. He ran his hands back up this body that he knew so well, but tonight it felt like he had never made love to her before. His eyes still watched hers as he felt her desire build when he touched certain parts of her body. When he got closer to her again, she undid his shirt, his belt, and his pants. She removed his shirt and let it drop to the floor. Then she pulled him close to her and she whispered ever so quietly, "I love you." She began kissing him slowly with light butterfly kisses. Then she made them longer and longer and more heated. She ran her hand through the hair on his chest and down his belly to the top of his jeans. She ran her hand over the top of his pants and felt his swollen desire through the heavy fabric. He let out an expressive moan as he fumbled with her bra. Once he got it off he sat up and picked Robin up and slid her panties off and pulled off his own jeans. Then he lay her down on the floor and kissed almost every inch of her body. She was glistening with the heat of her body and the need to be fulfilled. But Lee was making her wait and enjoying every second of the arousal. When he returned his face to hers they kissed long and hard again. Robin then returned the pleasures. She ran her hands through his hair, then up and down his back. She kissed his neck and nibbled on his ears, ran her tongue over his body, going further down his body, driving him to the point that he could no longer take it. He pulled her to him and lay on top of her and the two became one in an equally mutual desire of passion and need.

When they were both spent, they lay embraced in each other's arms for a long time. Finally Lee moved off of Robin and he kissed her and got up and went to the bathroom. Robin stood up and was gathering up their clothes and was going to take them to the bedroom. When Lee came back with a blanket and asked, "Where are you going? I got this so we could just lay here a little longer."

Robin felt he was almost begging her to not let this moment end.

"I'll be right back." She answered as she continued and went up the stairs. She wanted to put on the pink negligee set she had bought that afternoon. She threw the clothes on the floor and quickly went to her closet and put on the set. She brushed her hair and spritzed on some perfume, then went back to Lee.

"God, how can you get any more beautiful tonight? Where did you get that?"

"Thank-you. I bought it on impulse this afternoon. Do you like it?"

"Robin you look so good in pink. I love it. You know it reminds me of that pink nightie you wore when we first met, remember that? I used to think about you wearing that all the time, it drove me crazy."

Robin laughed.

"You know that's exactly what I thought when I saw it this afternoon and I just had to buy it. I wonder if it will stay on any longer than that other pink one ever did?"

"Well you know, if I had my way, I would keep you naked all the time. But I'm afraid I'm not as young as I was back then, so it may just be staying on for awhile."

They both laughed and Robin cuddled up in Lee's arms on the couch.

"Let's eat some of this dessert and perhaps we will build up some strength to do that again."

Robin lit the burner under the fondue pot and removed the plastic wrap from the fruit while Lee poured them each another glass of Grand Marnier.

Chapter Twenty-One

Lee threw as much of his stuff as he could in the back of his truck and drove away leaving a strip of rubber on the road. Robin remained in the bathroom crying.

"Shit, shit, shit. What a fuckin shit I am." Lee yelled at himself as he drove toward town.

"Where the fuck am I going to live?" He drove over to Joe's. No one was home.

"Maybe it's not a good idea to let anyone else know about this just yet." He thought. "But then again they all already know the other side of the story anyway. What the fuck? I'll just go to a hotel tonight and figure out what to do in the morning." He was going to stop at the first hotel he found, but then he remembered who he was and that he could probably stay anywhere he wanted. So he drove into town and found the Holiday Inn on the main drag and checked in. They had a great bar here. He knew that because he had played in it many times over the years. He asked who the bar manager was and it turned out it was still Frank Webster. He had been there years ago when Lee and the boys were just starting out. Lee checked in and took the small suitcase with his clothing and personal belongings to the room. He changed into jeans and a T-shirt and put on his old comfy cowboy boots, brushed his teeth and his hair, and went to the bar.

Frank recognized Lee right away and found him a seat at the bar off to the side so he wouldn't be too noticeable. He ordered himself a shot of tequila with a beer chaser. He felt like getting out of it tonight. The band was young and okay. Lee had seen better, but he had also seen much worse. Twice he got asked to dance, but he politely refused. He just sat at the bar and drank. Frank kept his eye on Lee. All Lee had said when he walked in was,

"I've got woman problems." Frank nodded his head. He had dealt with this many times before, but not with someone as well known as Lee Cotton. Finally Lee had relaxed a bit and went and danced with a pretty girl who had been watching him. They danced until closing time, he gave her a hug and kissed her good-night and was trying to talk her into going up to his room with him when Frank came along and changed Lee's plans. He escorted the young lady out and got one of the bouncers to take Lee to his room. When he walked into the room, Lee flopped down on the bed and passed out until one p.m. the next afternoon.

For the next six months this was how Lee spent most of his days and nights. When he was sober he felt so much pain that at least he had the insight to write it all down and he came up with some brilliantly emotional songs. He would spend days in his room writing and writing, and then he would send the lyrics to Robin. Then at night the band would be on the road somewhere and they would perform and Lee either had to drink or do some coke to make it through the night. The rule for the band was no drinking while performing, and that's when Lee discovered cocaine. No one else would know. He could just go off to the bathroom and no one would clue in. So, he became addicted for a short time. He would usually go do a line during a break, but after a while he couldn't even open without having something to get him through. The rest of the time he slept with any woman that would have him, which was usually a new one every night. He was a very good-looking man. He did not have any problem attracting women's attention although none of them meant anything to him, he kept hoping that eventually he would find one that made him feel the way Robin had. Every few weeks he called Robin collect from the road. She wouldn't accept the charges. He kept trying. He decided to send her pink roses once a month. She didn't respond to those either.

Robin on the other hand wasn't having the time of her life either. She had been extremely upset for a long time. She loved Lee more than anything in the world. He was her world. She had called her parents and they of course, were not surprised.

"Honey, the boy is in a band. What did you expect?"

So much for understanding from them. Lee's parents were more understanding. But, they weren't too surprised either.

"We knew this music business wasn't good for him, that it would ruin his life. And see, we were right."

Robin tried to convince them all that Lee was very talented at what he did. This was something that happened between them, not the music business. But that was something Robin had a hard time believing herself. She could not see Lee ever doing anything else. This was in his blood, but could she live with the fact that he could have any woman he wanted every single night of the week? Would she ever be enough for him? Would he always want more? Was she pretty enough for him? What if she didn't stay slim and attractive, would he leave? Would she ever be able to trust him again? It was all too much to think about. So she gave up thinking about it. She asked Jose and Maria for a leave of absence and she went to Mexico for three weeks by herself.

She drank lots of tequila and met people to party with every night. Being on her own, it was easy for people to approach her and she was easy to talk to. She was staying at a luxury resort in Cabo San Lucas, where she felt perfectly safe as she had told the management that she was alone, and they were very accommodating. She met a couple of men while she was there and she actually slept with both of them, which even to her was a shock. She didn't really want to, but she had had enough to drink that it just didn't matter.

The first time was the hardest because she still had feelings for Lee and she figured that the only way to get over them would be to get over him. So she had dinner with Steve and they danced and kissed. He was in Mexico for a convention. Robin never asked if he was single or married or even what his last name was. She didn't care. He was an okay guy, but he was too much into himself and Robin didn't like that. The sex was awful! Robin was used to passion with Lee. With this guy he wanted to prove that he was a great lover, but he did nothing but annoy Robin. When he finally finished pleasing himself he got up and left. Robin avoided him for the rest of the week.

The next guy was a great lover. His name was Vito. Maybe it was the Italian in him, but he was exactly what Robin needed. She told him that she was in the restaurant business and was single. She used her maiden name so as not to start any questions. It was just easier. He and a bunch of his friends were in Mexico for a week from California. He told her that he worked in the entertainment business. Robin had to watch what she said about that in order to avoid him asking her questions, she just asked him a lot of questions that she already knew the answers to. They ended up spending three nights and days together. It was nothing but great sex. They barely saw the light of day, which at the time was fine with Robin. She felt like she was perhaps getting even with Lee, she didn't know why but it was cleansing to her. They parted without any commitments or need to keep in touch. It was never even brought up. She did realize however that although Vito was fun, he wasn't Lee. There was just something that they had that Robin had never felt with anyone else. And she doubted she ever would find that something again.

It had been about four months that they had been apart and Robin knew exactly where Lee and the band were all the time.

The wives all kept in touch and they all took turns filling Robin in on how Lee was falling apart and into booze and drugs. Robin figured they were blowing this way out of proportion because she couldn't imagine Lee doing drugs. The band and his music were too important to him. He was still sending her lyrics to songs that he had written and before she knew it, they were hits on the radio. He still sent her roses once a month. She still avoided contact with him. Partly because now she knew how badly she needed him and that they were meant for each other, and partly because she didn't quite know what to do about it. Could she just call him up and say they needed to talk, to work things out? No she wouldn't. He had hurt her, he cheated on her, the worse thing that can happen between two people. But was it? But what if, but if only, but maybe……Oh God? Help me there are so many buts

When Robin went back to work after Mexico, she told Jose and Maria that it was time for a change for her. She needed to get on with her life and she didn't know what it would be but it was time to move on. They understood and let Robin choose her replacement, whom she spent the next month training, and planning for a future of her own.

Robin was packing up the remainder of her and Lee's stuff from the house they'd rented. She decided it was time to move to someplace smaller. She was going to take all Lee's things to his parent's house and move herself closer to the city. She didn't want to move too far away from Jose and Maria because they were her family here and she needed them, and they needed her too. She had the stereo cranked as she was cleaning and packing, when she heard the doorbell and loud knocks. She turned down the stereo, went to the door and flung it open expecting it to be the next door neighbor complaining about the noise. It was Lee.

He looked like hell. Robin fought the urge to run into his arms. She had never seen him look like this. He had lost a bunch of weight, his beautiful hair was limp and stringy. He was smoking a cigarette.

"Hi Rob. Can I come in?"

"Sure." She moved away from the door and gestured for him to enter.

"Are you moving?" He asked, in a sad tone as he walked through the doorway.

"Yes. It's time to get on with my life and I thought this would be a good place to start."

"Where are you going to go?"

"I thought closer to the city and someplace smaller. I don't need this much room. I have your stuff packed. I was going to take it to your parent's place for you. I hope that would be alright with you."

She looked up from the floor that she had been staring at since he came in.

"Yeah, that would be fine. You look great Rob, you have a tan. Have you been away?" His eyes looked questioningly into hers.

"Uh huh. I spent three weeks in Mexico about a month ago. The tan is almost gone now."

"Wow, good for you. Who did you go with?"

"No one."

"Really? That's not like you."

"I know. I needed to be alone with my thoughts and I couldn't go home, you know, they just wouldn't understand. Besides Mexico was closer, so I just went."

"Did you have any good thoughts while you were there?" He looked at Robin with a plea for help in his eyes.

"Maybe." She replied with the first sparkle that she had had in her eyes for a very long time. "Do you want a cup of coffee or something to drink?"

"Yeah, a beer would be great, if you've got one."

"I don't think I do." She lied. She didn't like the looks of him. She could tell he had been drinking far too much for several nights.

"Anything else?"

"Coffee will be fine then."

"Well come to the kitchen with me and I'll have one too."

He followed her into the kitchen looking at the boxes of their life she had packed up.

"When are you out of here?"

"Not until the end of the month. Two more weeks. But I'm not working right now so I have lots of time to get things organized."

"Did you take some time off work?" He asked with a concerned look on his face.

"Yeah, you could say that."

"Robin what's going on with you? I thought your job was the most important thing to you."

"Well it was, but something else is now." She looked at him with a hint of a smile on her face.

"Oh........Maybe I'd better leave." He stood up and started for the front door.

Robin grabbed his arm and said,

"Please don't leave, we need to talk."

They sat and talked all night. There were angry words and lots of tears from both of them. They both spilled their guts with the pain they had both been through. Lee could not stop apologizing for what he had done. They both knew that what they had was something very special and it was not something that a lot of people, even any of the other people that they knew, had. It was soul deep and they were truly sole mates. Two people who belonged together. They drank a couple of pots of coffee, ordered pizza for dinner and talked more. By the time morning had arrived, they had come to several conclusions and were both dead tired. The exhaustion and relief from finally dealing with all that they had gone through and all the things that needed to be said to each other. So with a final reckoning and realization that they could never be apart again they climbed into their old bed together and instantly fell asleep.

Robin woke first, sometime in the late afternoon. She looked over at Lee, who looked like he hadn't slept this well in weeks. He didn't have the painful look he had on his face when he had arrived the previous afternoon. They had decided that they could work all this out. And since Robin was no longer working, she would be able to be on the road with Lee. And they would buy their own house so they could have something to look forward to coming home to. And perhaps, one day soon they would start a family. Robin knew in her heart that this was good, and right and everything would be fine now. She forgave Lee for sleeping with Jennifer, and as she explained, even though it took a lot of time and thinking and tequila, she told him she finally did understand why it happened. She told him she had slept with someone in Mexico. He was surprised, but also relieved. He said he could not apologize enough for what he had put them both through. And he swore over and over again that he would make this up to her for the rest of his life.

Chapter Twenty-Two

The next morning was beautiful, hot and sunny when the Cotton's awoke at nine a.m. This would be their last day together for the next three months and they had a lot to do. Last night, they had made enough love to get them through being apart for a few months. But they knew it was going to be different this time. Lee knew it was strictly business and he could deal with it that way. He was concerned though about Robin wanting to stay at home. He had gotten used to her being along and it made being in a new city fun because she always made sure they did as much sightseeing as their schedule would allow. She always researched a city before they got there so she had the days they were available, booked with places to see. They did have to fit in personal appearances and do radio promos. Sometimes that was all the time they would have in a city. But she always went along. She would always get the guys to autograph a stack of photos ahead of time and she would hand them out to the people at the back who couldn't get close enough for autographs. She helped with the selling of the T-shirts and souvenirs just for something to do. She usually got a rush from the audience's energy and enjoyed the show more when she was involved with the crowd. Other times if there was more than one show in the same city, the wives would go out shopping or for dinner or even to a movie and miss the band perform.

Robin, finally, wasn't concerned at all this time about Lee going. In fact she was looking forward to it. Amazing how a couple of weeks away talking to old friends can make your whole life change. Not that it was her whole life, but she finally felt she was where she should be and her life was great the way it was. And she knew deep in her heart that Lee loved her as much as he loved his music, which Robin knew was more than anything else in the world. She also knew that nothing would come between them again. They had the kind of love that books and movies and songs are written about. Robin knew this for a fact because many of 'Rocket Fuels' top hits were written about their life. How many people have spouse's who not only write a number one song about them but also sing it to the whole world. She laughed to herself looking back just a couple of days ago in Victoria, how she had been feeling then compared to now. "I guess I've really grown up, and it took going back twenty years to do it."

Robin put on a pot of coffee and whipped up a batch of carrot muffins, they were Lee's favorite. They would have a quick breakfast, and get everything in order. Half an hour later they were eating hot muffins and drinking fresh brewed coffee.

Lee glanced up over the morning paper and asked,

"What should we start with today Hon?"

Robin looked up from the newspaper that she was reading and replied,

"I don't care. All I really have to do is go to the cleaners to pick up your stage clothes and dress shirts. Is there anything else that needs to be done around here that you haven't told me about?"

"No, I think everything is under control. Besides, our Dads' know more about what goes on around here than either of us do." They laughed, knowing he was right.

"Ok then, I guess if it's alright with you I'll hang with you all day and help get the bus ready. Do you want me to cook anything special to take with you?"

"Everything! You know better than to ask that. It's really weird being married to a chef and eating some of the crappy food we eat on the road. That's what I think I'm going to miss the most about you not coming along this time. I'm going to be eating 'Road Food'. You won't be there to cook for us."

"Thanks a lot! All you're going to miss about me not coming is the cooking! Well then I think I'm not going to cook anything, just so you will appreciate me more when you get home!" She stuck her tongue out at him and laughed.

"Actually you can take the rest of these muffins but that's about it Pal, you can just wait till you get home." She stood up and went to the fridge to put away the cream. "Oh look, you can take the rest of this roast too. There now I don't feel so bad." She found a box of plastic wrap and wrapped up the roast and then the muffins.

"I guess then we should stop at the grocery store so I can grab a few things to have till we make the next stop. Did all the laundry get done? I want those old blue jeans and my black sweats. I need some clean underwear too and...."

Robin interrupted, "Relax Lee. Just because I'm not going with you doesn't mean I haven't packed for you. It's pretty much done. All the regular stuff. I bought you a new toothbrush and some deodorant. They are in your shaving kit. Anything else out of the ordinary you can get for yourself! I've got to have a quick shower then we can get going. You better call our parents and say good-bye, you probably won't have any other time today and you'll be leaving too early in the morning to do it then." She left the kitchen to go have a shower.

Lee put down the paper and picked up the phone. He called Robin's family first. Her Dad answered and Lee did the usual good-bye, take care of things while we are gone speech, but this time he added,

"Take care of Robin for me too Dad. I'm going to miss

her." Then he called his parents. They both got on a phone and went through the good-byes. His Dad went through all the stuff he was planning to do while Lee was away and his Mother kept saying, "You be good son. Make sure the bus driver drives carefully. We'll see you at Christmas son."

"Christmas? Christmas? I won't be home until Christmas? God that feels like forever", he thought.

Robin came walking down the hall just then all showered and wearing her comfortable jeans and a 'Rocket Fuel' fall tour T-shirt.

"Do you know I won't be home until Christmas?" He watched Robin pull on her blue cowboy boots.

"Yes. What's the matter with you? You're not usually this messed up when you go away."

"I don't know, I guess being on vacation for a couple of weeks just.....I don't know, I lost all track of time and I guess I just haven't had time to get psyched up yet. I know I haven't checked the tour schedule yet. I hope that manager of ours is on top of things because I haven't had a chance to look at any of that stuff."

"Honey relax. That's why Ben gets the big bucks you pay him. He will have taken care of everything you know that. And that's why I am going to be busy while you're gone. I would like to have everything done and ready for a nice big family Christmas at home this year. Remember last year we had to have Christmas in Nashville and you guys did all those special shows? So this year I think it's our turn to have everyone at our house. Besides all us wives are looking forward to having you guys home. But it's still a few months away. I'll be working on it all from here and we can talk about it over the phone when the time gets closer. All you have to do is have a spectacular performance each night and make lots of money so you can buy me a really great Christmas gift!" She had walked over to Lee and wrapped her arms around his neck and played with his hair as she talked. Then she leaned her forehead against his and kissed the end of his nose.

"Don't I always get you a great Christmas gift?" He asked pretending to be kind of hurt.

"Always! You always get the best gifts silly. I know you won't forget to this year either. So let's get on with this day, we've got things to do."

"Do you want to go on the Harley or in the truck?"

"We can't go on the Harley, you have to take all your stuff. Let's take my car. It needs to be run. It hasn't been driven for weeks. I'll go start it, while you get your things together. Let's go!"

The Porsche started right up for Robin. She revved the engine up for a couple of minutes and then backed the car out of the garage and pulled up along the side of the house. The five-stall garage was not attached to the house. It was set off to the left. In between the garage and the house was a huge paved interlocking brick driveway-parking area with a long curvy driveway that winded it's way to the road. A white board fence ran down the length of the drive with lots of wild flowers growing in beds between the road and the fence. The house was built right on the edge of a small hill so the front yard gently rolled away from the house. Lee and Robin had designed the house themselves, and it was far bigger than they would ever need, but they had far more money than they would ever need as well. So they decided that a beautiful home would be their investment for the future. They also knew they could be done in this business tomorrow.

The house was an eclectic combination of country, traditional, modern contemporary and a bit of Tex-Mex. The outside had a modern contemporary look. The front was light colored brick with ivory stucco and cream wood trim. It had a grand front entrance, with the same paving stones as the driveway going in a wide path to the front door. Surrounding the front doorway were lots of huge plants, a water fountain and a spectacular lighting display that came on at dusk. There were double front doors with oval shaped etched glass in each panel. Entering through those doors you came to a huge foyer with a closet for coats to the right and the 'Party Room' (traditionally called the Parlor) to the left. This room was used when they entertained formally. It was quite big and was decorated a little more modern than the rest of the house. It had a wet bar and a fully stocked liquor cabinet that ran the length of the back wall, six black leather couches around the edges of the room and hardwood floors to dance on. The coffee and end tables were smoked glass, and there were lots of bouquets of silk flower, which were replaced with real fresh flowers when they entertained or were going to be at home for any length of time. There were several pieces of art on the walls they had picked up somewhere on the road. Robin tried to collect something from every city or town they went to. She always wrote the country or city and the date of purchase on a piece of paper and taped it to the back or bottom of each item. Mainly this room housed all the awards, gold and platinum records, and the band's memorabilia they had received over the years. Robin always felt this room was too formal and cold and had wanted to redecorate it, but had never got around to it.

Down the hall was the powder room and the hallway continued to the huge dining room. This room was designed to hold a table that would seat twenty-four people. Between the band members, the crew and their families the room would be full. And when Lee and Robin's own families were all together, they too could fill the room. This room was a more contemporary décor. The table was custom made from oak and was finished in a whitewashed shade of ivory with matching high back chairs. Robin had collected two different sets of china, all with matching accompaniment sets, complete sets of crystal stemware and gold-plated cutlery for twenty-four along with a large assortment of lace and different colored table linens. She had many different sets of candleholders, vases, and an elaborate collection of serving platters and serving bowls. All of these items were at home in a wall to wall, floor to ceiling built-in china cabinet that was made from oak and stained the same color as the table and chairs. Everything was perfectly organized and Robin liked it that way.

This room, as well as the kitchen, living room, and family room were all done in shades of ivories and off whites. For special occasions and especially at Christmas, Robin used lots of gold and red colors in these rooms.

Through a doorway off the dining room was Robin's favorite room, the kitchen. The kitchen was the room Robin had worked on the most. She knew exactly what she had wanted and needed and how it would be set up to be an excellent working, everyday eating, and entertaining room. When they were at home, this was where they spent the most time, so Robin wanted it to be extremely comfortable and functional. The appliances were all industrial style. A stainless steel commercial range with six burners, two full-sized ovens with warming drawers. The biggest Sub-Zero refrigerator they could get with the freezer section on the bottom, a wine fridge and a second refrigerator just for beer, which constantly needed to be filled. A large L shaped island went through the center of the room. Four people could sit at the end of it. The remainder was where Robin would prepare food. All of her baking supplies were stored together in huge slide out drawers under the prep area. The countertops were all black granite and the floors were white Mexican tile. Her well used sets of copper pots looked quite at home in the glassed door cupboards that surrounded the range. The kitchen was an eclectic mix of contemporary, tying it to the dining room, and a little country to go with the views of the country from this room, to some wild Tex-Mex that was just a part of Texas life, which ended up flowing into the adjoining family-fun room. The cabinets were all finished in the same whitewashed oak that were in the dining room, with gold and crystal handles. The kitchen was the center of the main floor of the house and all the other rooms branched off of it. It was almost a semi-circle. The one back wall consisted of a double set of French doors that led out onto a deck and then down a couple of stairs to the in-ground pool. A professional gardener looked after the perfectly manicured lawns and gardens. He charged a fortune for his work, but it was worth it to them because they were never around long enough to take proper care of everything and the gardens were too much to expect their parents to look after on top of everything else they did around the ranch.

The family room, (or as Lee called it "The fun room") was Lee's favorite room in the house. It was where everyone could relax, kick up their feet and have a cold beer while listening to any kind of music on the stereo that Lee was constantly upgrading or adding new components to. The entire house was wired for sound and this room was "Grand Central Music". Music could be turned on in every room in the house as well as the outside decks and pool areas. Or just in one room alone. The bedroom could suddenly have very romantic music playing with the flick of the remote. The collection of music was huge and a lot of the CDs had never even been listened to. This was usually due to lack of time being at home. There was also a big screen television in this room. Football games on Monday nights were a tradition in this room when they were at home. There was always an open door policy, Lee and Robin never knew who or how many people would be showing up from week to week. That was part of the fun. Robin would always prepare a ton of food, and sometimes there were fifty people, sometimes just the two of them. If no one showed up the food was lunch for the ranch hands the next day or frozen to be used the next week. Being a good ol' Texas boy, Lee's favorite team was the Dallas Cowboys and although Troy was very cute and a good friend, Robin's favorite team was San Francisco. Her Dad got her hooked when she was young and she really liked Joe Montana back then, so she still kept loyal for her Dad's sake. She would cheer for Dallas when they were playing any other team. Needless to say, this room was very comfortable with six overstuffed couches, two in bright floral's, two in black and two in beige. They were arranged in a semi-circle in front of the television for viewing nights. There were also six overstuffed armchairs and a stack of assorted patterned floor cushions that were scattered around the room. The furniture arrangement was changing from week to week in this room. The room was on an angle from the front of the house looking almost like a separate building. One complete wall was windows with another set of French doors in the middle of all the windows that opened onto a small closed in deck filled with plants, and several wooden deck chairs. This area was used for smoking, as Robin would not allow smoking in the house. The doors also allowed in a nice breeze on hot summer nights. The white tile floor from the kitchen met up with black carpet in the fun room. A fireplace was along the wall opposite the television, so after a game or if it wasn't a t.v. night, they could rearrange the furniture and sit and listen to music while watching the fire. There was a lot of modern art in this room. There were two sets of stairs between the fun room and the dining room. One set led to the upper floor and the other to the recording studio that took over the entire basement.

Upstairs were four bedrooms, laundry room, library and office.

The master suite was decorated in pinks and blues. It had a fireplace, huge ensuite with a Jacuzzi tub and a separate steam shower. Robin and Lee each had their own walk in closets, with dressing areas and full length mirrors. There was another set of French doors that opened onto a good-sized deck that over looked the entire ranch, the pool area and yard below.

Each of the other bedrooms was set up with Queen sized beds and fine oak furniture. All with their own adjoining bathrooms. Overnight guests were always welcomed and encouraged to stay here.

The office was the manly room in the house. Decorated in forest green and beige's with a huge oak desk that Robin had bought at an auction in Dallas and had refinished. The floors were carpeted in thick forest green, with ivory walls with a wallpaper border around the top of horses grazing in fields. The walls were covered in pictures of Lee and Robin's life together at various events since they had met. In this room all the important papers were filed, bills got dealt with, mail was brought here to be sorted as it was opened, the answering machine was in here so that messages could be dealt with promptly. Another set of doors opened out onto a balcony that had two cape-cod chairs painted in forest green and a small table to place morning coffee or afternoon lunch to allow for a break and some fresh air if the workload was too heavy in the room.

Across the hall from the office was the library. Robin and Lee both loved to read and they both kept every book they had ever read, so they had to have a room to store them all in. Every wall was floor to ceiling bookshelves. The only windows in the room were on one wall, high up and they were half circles. Two black leather recliners sat precariously in the middle of the room each with their own end tables and reading lights. It actually looked like a very stuffy room, needless to say it wasn't used much other than to store or retrieve books.

Lee collected the garment bags and suitcases he had packed and carried them downstairs and went to get the food Robin had said he could take. He did one last quick look through his duffel bag and made sure he had his wallet and a book to read, his shaving kit and his favorite shampoo! He hated being on the road and not being able to get his hair just right. Robin had everything ready like she always did. 'Boy', he thought to himself, 'I'm really going to miss having her along. Now it will be just like work and I won't be able to wait till I can get home.' He picked everything up in one big armful and pulled the back door shut with his foot as he went out. They managed to fit everything into the Porsche. Robin drove.

A half-hour later they were at the warehouse. Robin helped Lee carry his things to the bus. Everyone but Billy was there. The girls all hugged. Ashley and Becky were going to meet the guys in New York in two weeks for the weekend on the East Coast part of the tour. It was the wrong time of the year to be travelling to the East Coast, but the demand was there and they hadn't been east for two years. Now was the time. The new album had just been released and touring was necessary to promote it. They would start in New York and head up to Boston, then to Maine, over to the first Canadian stop, Toronto. After that they would cover eleven states in seventy-eight days. Not only doing shows, but also radio promos, local television stations, free mini concerts, and autograph sessions. There wasn't going to be much free time. The last concert date would be in early December, so they would all be home in plenty of time for Christmas.

Virginia, who had three children, two that were in school, was staying home, and so was Sue, who had two little ones at home. They had just been away from their kids for the two weeks with Robin in Victoria so both of them knew they had to stay put for this tour. Robin would spend time with them while she was home too.

Everyone was catching up with small talk when Billy showed up alone. The girls all asked for Becky. He said she was at home preparing a nice dinner they could have together when he got home. All the other wives had the same plans for the evening, but it would be an early night as the bus was leaving at four a.m. That meant up at three a.m. at least. The rules were if you weren't there when the bus left, it was your responsibility to get your own transportation to the next gig on your own. Many times over the years, each of them had missed the bus for lots of different reasons, but to date, no one had missed a gig. That was a good thing. No matter how irresponsible they had been during their careers, they all respected their professions enough to not screw up the gigs. And they all meant a lot to each other. They were a team. They had all fought over the years, for all kinds of reasons, booze, drugs, women, who's songs were better then someone else's, why did he get to sleep in the big bunk? who drank the last beer?, why does his wife always come along?, why does he always get the first pick of the food?, etc, etc, etc. But, inspite of it all, they had all remained loyal friends through the good, the bad and even the ugly!

The two semis were loaded with all the equipment, stage lighting, and everything else needed for the tour. The drivers had just received the final checklist and were about to start up the engines and get on the road. It was faster and easier for the semis to travel at night. Less traffic, and less delays. They had to be on location long before the guys arrived, just to make sure everything was there and to allow time for the roadies to set up. Now and then it happened that there were malfunctions with equipment or things were forgotten or got left behind. This allowed time to get it fixed before the show.

Robin excused herself and went and found Lee loading his clothes into the drawer that was his. When Robin went with him they would ride on the bus most of the time. Other times they would rent a car and meet up with the rest of the band in the city they were due to be in. Occasionally Robin would have to sleep in Lee's bunk with him, but normally they would get a hotel room so they could have privacy.

"I guess I'll be sleeping on the bus this whole trip. Boy it's been a long time since I've been the one to do a whole trip on the bus."

"Oh Honey, it will be good for you. You know, get you back in touch with the way it used to be and why you enjoy this business so much."

"Yeah right!" Lee turned to look into Robin's eyes. "I'm really going to miss you. You have no idea how much."

"I know we've been over this and I'm going to miss you just as much, but let's keep focused. It's your job, and I have one at home that needs to be taken care of. And I want us to have a great Christmas. So I need all this time to plan and cook and shop. You'll see. It will go so fast. Can we go home now? We only have a few hours left together."

"Sure, I'm pretty much done."

Lee went and talked to the other guys and they too were getting ready to head home for the night. Everyone said their good-byes and see you in the mornings.

Chapter Twenty-Three

After a pretty much sleepless night, Robin rolled over when the alarm went off at two-fifty a.m.

"You awake Honey?" she asked as she patted Lee's arm.

"Yeah, I have been for awhile." Lee rolled over to Robin and wrapped her in his arms. "Can we make love before I have to leave?"

"Of course." Robin replied. She began kissing him. They made love but it wasn't passionate, it was more like a need that had to be filled. It was like they had to fill each other up with a part of themselves because they would be apart for a long time and this would be what would hold them close to each other for the next few months.

When Robin climbed out of bed she felt like being sick. She didn't realize how much this was affecting her. She didn't want Lee to see her fall apart in front of him, so she quickly turned on the shower and climbed in and put her face up to the stream of water so he wouldn't notice the tears streaming out of her eyes. Lee climbed in behind her and wrapped his arms around her trembling body. He didn't seem to notice that she was trembling, she said she was cold so he reached over and turned up the hot water. They each cleansed their bodies and washed their hair, clinging to each moment they still had together. They dried off and Robin dressed and was planning to cook Lee breakfast, but they had run out of time. It was time to leave. Lee wanted Robin to take the Explorer. He didn't want her driving the Porsche alone at this time of night. So, quietly, they left the ranch. The sun wasn't even close to rising yet and Lee took a look around property that was shimmering with the night lighting effects the gardener had put in in the spring.

"The place sure does look pretty doesn't it?"

"Yes it does. But take a good look now, because when you come home you won't even recognize the place. I'm going to have Christmas decorations everywhere!" Robin was trying to change the mood. They both were feeling sad. She wanted to make everything light and have something to look forward to because she would start to cry soon enough. She at least wanted to get to the bus before Lee had to see the tears.

They made it. As Lee turned into the lot she looked over at him. He was looking at her.

"What?" she asked.

"Nothing. I just want to look at you a little while longer." He put his arm over the back of the seat to pull her a little closer. "You know, it feels like we've never been apart before. It feels like the first time we've left each other."

"I know. I feel it too. It's just that for the last four or five years we have been together all the time. I guess that maybe that wasn't a good thing because now it hurts too much......" She couldn't finish what she was going to say because she had started to cry.

Lee turned off the engine and pulled Robin into his arms.

"God, I hate to see you cry. You know, there is no reason you can't come. It was all your decision not to in the first place. Why don't you come with Becky and Ash and meet us in New York? You know you could do some great shopping there!" He put his hand under Robin's chin and got her to look into his eyes.

"No. I can't understand why I'm being so emotional about this. But I'm not going to come with you and I'm not going to meet you. I really think that we do need this time apart. It may not seem like it right now, but it will be better when you get back."

Everyone else was starting to arrive. Robin dried her tears and they both climbed out of the truck to say good morning to the rest of the gang. Steve, the bus driver had been there for awhile and had done the pre-trip test and had the bus warmed up. The semis had left the night before. All that was left was for the women to leave and the tour to begin. It was three-fifty-five. The bus would leave in five minutes. Everyone coupled off and said their own private good-byes then they did a group hug and the guys started to climb aboard. Lee grabbed Robin's hand and pulled her close to him one last time.

"I love you sweetheart." He kissed her gently on the lips.

"I love you more." She whispered back as their hands slowly separated and just their fingers touched.

"Good-bye." They both said at the same time. Lee ran and jumped through the bus door just as it was about to close. Everyone waved good-bye and the bus drove away.

The girls all hugged and said their own good-byes, promising to be in touch in a day or two. Robin climbed into the Explorer. She watched Virginia and Sue leave and wondered how they were so calm. They both had kids at home to deal with and they had been at home a lot more than Robin had. As she started up the truck to head home, she wondered if they had felt this way the first time they had been apart from their husbands for any length of time. She made a mental note to ask them when she saw them next.

When Robin arrived home the sun still wasn't up so she decided to climb back in bed herself. She took off her clothes and climbed under the covers. She awoke just before noon. She lay in bed for the longest time trying to decide what to do. Finally, she got up and went downstairs and put on a pot of coffee. She decided to call her Mom while the coffee was brewing.

"Hi Mom. Yeah he got away just fine. I'm ok. I just don't know what to do with myself first." Her mother told her just to take it easy today, settle in and relax before taking on anything big. As she poured herself a cup of coffee and made some toast, she decided to take Ginger for a ride and then come in and go through all the mail and correspondence they had avoided the last couple of weeks. Robin poured the last of her coffee down the sink and went out to the barn. She tacked up Ginger and they set out to check on the ranch. Robin started off with a slow walk for about twenty minutes then she kicked Ginger into a full gallop. The two of them looked like a beautiful picture, both of their blonde hair flowing behind them as they toured the property. Two hours later they returned to the barn at a very gentle walk. Robin removed the saddle and bridle and gave Ginger a great rub down and grooming, filled the manger with hay and went back to the house. She realized that all the fresh air had made her hungry as well. She found some yogurt and a banana, then poured herself a glass of milk and took it all up to the office to begin catching up.

As she sat down and took a bite of the banana, she looked at the answering machine, the lighted display said they had twenty-seven messages waiting.

"Oh my God. I thought Lee checked these the other day." Robin said out loud. She found a pen and a note-book and hit the play button on the machine. The first call was from Jose, wanting to know where they were and for them to please call him when they could. The next one was from Lee's dentist saying it was time for him to go in for a check-up. Sterling Parker, their lawyer, asking Lee to call back. A neighbor inviting them to a barbecue. A couple of business calls. Sterling Parker again, asking Lee to call back as soon as possible. Robin's doctor's office, saying that she was now three months overdue for her annual physical check-up and this would be the last reminder call they would make. Chet calling from the bar. A couple of calls were from friends inviting them to parties and dinners, Robin's brother calling to say Hi. Sterling Parker again, saying that this was a very urgent matter that had to be dealt with immediately. A few more business calls. Marty calling to say that Pam had gone into labor two days after they had left. That would be yesterday Robin figured.

"Oh God, please let Pam and the baby be alright." She prayed.

And the last two calls were from one of Lee's brothers and Robin's Mom, both from today.

"Who do I call first?" Robin thought as she went over the list. Sterling was far too intense so whatever he wanted was probably not as important as he made it sound. Robin decided to call Marty first.

She got the answering machine. The message said,

"We have a new baby! If you would like more information please call 555-8367." Robin laughed. Trust Marty, always making people smile. She dialed the number.

"Hi Marty, it's Robin. What's going on? Is Pam ok?"

"Hi Robin, thanks for calling back. Yes Pam is just fine. We have a new little daughter to tell you about. She came about three weeks early, but everyone is doing fine."

Robin could hear the joy in Marty's voice and her eyes began to well up with tears.

"Oh Marty, Congratulations! I'm so happy for you guys. Now you have a complete family, one of each, that is so nice. What are you going to name her? How much did she weigh? Come on I need all the information."

"Pam's sitting right here I'll let her tell you everything else. Good to hear from you Robin. Talk to you soon."

"Bye Marty. Hi Momma, how are you?"

"Hi Robin, I'm doing fine. This is much harder the second time around at my age." She said laughing.

"Come on I need all the good stuff, what did you name her?"

"Delany Robin Rose. Six pounds nine ounces. Not much hair, but I think perhaps blonde right now, her eyes look very dark. It's too soon to tell exactly. She at least let me go to the reunion before she graced us with her presence. Now I'm back to sleepless nights and enjoying every precious second of it!"

"I'm very touched that you used my name."

"Well I hoped you wouldn't mind and since you're not having any kids you needed to have someone to carry on that pretty name and besides you mean a lot to me too." They were both in tears now.

"Pam I wish I was there, I'd give you a big hug."

"I know you would, but you see, now I can come there sooner. I'm hoping that if you don't mind and everything goes all right with us, that we could come spend your Thanksgiving with you, since Lee is away. I know you have lots of family, but I also know you will need a distraction or you will be missing him too much."

"That would be wonderful. I can't wait."

"Besides, I figured I'm not going to be doing much cooking for the next while, so in a couple of months my family could really use a great home cooked meal!" They were both laughing again and Robin could hear the sounds of a new baby crying in the background.

"She's saying Hi Aunty Robin, I'll see you soon."

"I'm going to let you go Pam, take lots of pictures and call me when you can in a couple of days. I won't call you in case your busy, but I will be working on plans for Thanksgiving. Take care. Say Hi to big brother Jordan. Bye now. Talk to you soon." Robin hung up the phone and let her hand remain on the receiver for a few moments. She was on the verge of tears. She didn't know if they were for joy or jealousy.

The next call Robin made was to Sterling Parker.

Chapter Twenty-Four

"Hello Robin. Thank you for calling, but I'm afraid that it's Lee I need to talk to. I have an urgent matter to discuss with him."

"Well, Sterling, I'm afraid you've just missed him. He's just left for a three month tour and he won't be home until just before Christmas."

"Oh my God. I've been trying to reach him for days. Robin this is very urgent and time is of the essence, I must talk to Lee."

Robin was rolling her eyes, everything was urgent to Sterling. Robin figured that the only reason Lee kept him as their lawyer was because he was an old friend of the family. She knew that he wasn't up on Lee's music business and all the little side business ventures they dabbled in were beyond what Sterling should be involved with. He did a good job with what he understood and sent the rest to colleagues and then gave his lectures about being cautious and getting him to check everything before they got too involved.

"Now Sterling, I'm sure I can handle whatever needs to be taken care of...."

He interrupted,

"No Robin this is a personal matter that I need to discuss with Lee."

"Sterling you know that Lee and I discuss everything, I'm sure I can handle it and if I can't, Lee will be calling in a couple of days, I can explain it to him and call you back."

"I'm afraid we don't have a couple of days. I've only got about eighteen hours left. I have to have a response from Lee before nine a.m. tomorrow morning."

"Can you give me an idea what this is all about?"

"No, it's a private matter."

Robin was wondering to herself what could be so private that Lee hadn't discussed with her. Did he not have enough life insurance? Were they broke? Maybe he had done his Christmas shopping via Sterling?

"Sterling, give me a clue here please and perhaps I can help."

"I can't Robin. Don't you know where Lee is right now? You must have an itinerary, or some way of getting hold of him. Doesn't he have a cell phone?"

Robin was beginning to get annoyed.

"Yes he has a cell phone, but he only turns it on when he's making calls, he doesn't like to be disturbed. And," Robin began to giggle, "he usually leaves an itinerary, but I guess there wasn't enough time. We've only been home for three days. We went to Victoria for my high school reunion and we took a couple of weeks off. There was so much to do when we got home it must have been forgotten about. He told me that he wouldn't call tonight, but he will call tomorrow. That's the best I can do for you Sterling."

There was a moment of silence on the other end of the phone.

"Sterling.....are you there?"

"Robin," the tone had calmed in his voice and it sounded like he was going to bear bad news. "I have no other choice then. I need to see you as soon as possible."

They made arrangements. Sterling was going to drive out to the ranch. It would take him an hour from town. So Robin invited him to stay for dinner. It was already after four. She had time to go have a quick shower and get cleaned up before he would arrive. As she was taking off her riding clothes she couldn't stop thinking what this was all about.

"If Sterling is making a big deal out of nothing here, I'm going to be so pissed off." She quickly washed herself and got out of the shower and pulled on a beige pair of jeans and an ivory blouse. She lightly applied a small amount of make-up. As she looked at herself in the mirror she noticed how the fresh air of the days ride had made her face glow. She pulled her long hair up into a loose bun, then went downstairs to the kitchen to prepare something for dinner.

All she could find in the fridge were some vegetables. She began to prepare them for a vegetable pasta in a white wine sauce. She was going to pour herself a glass of wine while she was cooking but decided to wait until Sterling could join her. There was leftover chocolate sauce so she prepared some fruit for dessert.

It was five thirty on the clock in the kitchen when the front doorbell rang. Robin hadn't even heard Sterling's car pull up. She put down the spoon she was using to stir the sauce and went to answer the door. For all the years they had known Sterling, it made Robin laugh that he always came to the front door. Everyone else who knew them well came through the back.

"Good evening Sterling." Robin greeted as she opened the door.

Sterling stood with a somber look on his face and a large manila folder in his hand. He gave Robin a hug with his empty hand and followed her into the house.

"Come on in, can I get you a drink?" They walked into the family room and Sterling hadn't said a word.

"Would you like something to drink Sterling?" Robin asked again. A little louder this time.

"Scotch on the rocks would be fine. Robin, I think that perhaps I should not have accepted dinner. I hope you haven't gone to a lot of trouble. But we need to deal with this issue right now."

Robin went to the bar and poured the drink.

"Should I be pouring myself one too." She asked with a giggle in her voice, trying hard to not take Sterling too serious.

"Yes, I think you should."

Robin looked directly at Sterling. She was now feeling a little worried, something was wrong. She went to the kitchen and turned off the elements on the stove. She decided to wait to hear what Sterling had to say before she poured herself a drink. He had taken a seat in the dining room and placed his manila folder in front of himself. He pulled the chair out beside him and directed Robin to sit in it.

"Robin this is very difficult for me to be telling you. This is a very tragic turn of events and I've never had to deal with anything like this before in my career."

Robin interrupted,

"Is Lee okay?" Her voice was trembling.

"Yes, yes, he's fine. Perhaps I should get right to it." He stood up and like a lawyer in court, he folded his hands behind his back and began to pace the dining room floor as he spoke.

"Do you remember when you and Lee were separated a few years back?"

Robin nodded her head and kept her eyes glued to Sterling.

"Could you tell me why you separated?"

"Lee had a fling with another woman." Robin stated.

"Alright so you know that then. I didn't know how much you knew and I didn't want to be the one to tell you."

"Please continue." Robin begged.

Sterling put one of his hands on top of Robins,

"Dear, please bear with me as I explain. It turned out that the woman got pregnant and had a daughter."

Robin gasped and pulled her hand to her mouth.

"She contacted Lee only to tell him that he had a child. She didn't want anything from him just the knowledge that he would know there was a child in the world that was his. Of course, Lee being Lee he needed to make sure that they were both taken care of. He never had any contact with the woman or even saw the child. I handled everything for him. The hospital bills were paid and I made sure they were adequately provided for each month with extras for birthdays and Christmas. In this folder I have pictures that were sent every so often, Lee has never seen any of them. He doesn't even know about them." Sterling paused to look at Robin. She was sitting very still with her eyes looking at the folder and her hands twisted together in her lap. The happy glow that was in her face when he arrived was gone.

"Now this is where things become complicated. Last week the mother of the child was killed in a car accident. She never married and she had no other family. The child has been staying with friends, but the mother's will states that in the event of her death, she would like the daughter to be with her natural father. That is Lee. I have to have papers signed for the morning as to whether you will be taking custody or if she needs to be put into foster care and then put up for adoption."

Robin had begun to cry. Her hands were covering her mouth. She didn't know what to think. Other than the fact that she felt like throwing up, she was numb. She looked up at Sterling and he sat down and put an arm around her shoulders in a form of comfort.

"I'm sorry to be telling you this Robin. But you see the urgency. I can't speak on Lee's behalf about this. This is something that the two of you needed to work out together and discuss and I'm sure it will bring up the past and some kind of feelings, but a child's life is at stake here and we are running out of time."

"What do you think Lee would do?" Robin asked through her tears.

"I don't honestly know Robin. He realized he, pardon me, 'screwed up' and he didn't want to lose you again. You know he loves you more than anything else in this world. And he didn't want to hurt you so he walked away, so to speak from this to be with you."

Robin began crying harder now. All these years they had tried to have children and Lee had a daughter who could have been a part of their lives. Now she would be. Robin decided right then that this was a gift from heaven. It was something that was meant to be, and she was going to make a decision that was going to change their lives.

"Sterling, no one else is going to have Lee's daughter. She will come and live with us. I will sign any papers that need to be signed."

"Whoa girl. Slow down there. This is something that the two of you need to discuss and decide together. I won't let you make this decision alone."

Robin had walked into the kitchen to get a box of Kleenex, as she was drying her eyes and blowing her nose, she said,

"I would like to get her here as soon as possible and I don't want Lee to know."

"Robin you need to think this through a little more. Perhaps I can stall a little bit longer. Until we can hear from Lee."

"We can't tell Lee, Sterling. If he finds out he will cancel the tour and come home. This is very important but he has contracts and fans waiting. You know that. I will call Jack and Val right now and we can explain this to them. After all they are the paternal grandparents. They are her next of kin after Lee so let's see what they say."

Robin called Lee's parents and they arrived in a matter of minutes. They said their hello's and Jack and Sterling shook hands.

"What seems to be the problem here Sterling? Robin sounded a might concerned on the phone, said it was urgent."

"Mom, Dad, first of all can I get you a drink? Robin looked and Jack and then at Val. They both shook their heads.

"Is Lee alright?" Val asked in a voice laced with concern.

"Yes, he's fine. But ..... I have something that Sterling thinks I shouldn't decide on alone and we can't get hold of Lee until tomorrow night..........so I need your help."

Lee's mother sighed with relief. Robin decided she needed that glass of wine now so she got herself a glass and put two empty glasses on the table and went to the liquor cabinet and got the bottle of Scotch for Sterling. She put the alcohol on the table and told them to help themselves if they liked. Then she proceeded with the story.

When she had finished, both Jack and Val sat there silent for a few moments. Jack responded first. He poured himself a glass of Scotch and said,

"I don't feel that Lee has any say in this decision. It should be up to Robin. After all, he has know about this child all these years and chosen to have no contact. And now for him to ask Robin to allow his 'Love Child' to come into her house, well, I just think that Robin should decide if she can love another woman's child without any influence from Lee."

Val looked at Jack in horror.

"How can you say that Jack?" I agree, but this is also Lee's child and our grandchild. And for us to allow someone else to raise her would be wrong."

"Hold on you two." Robin smiled as she raised her hands. "I have already told Sterling that I would sign any papers and that no one else is going to raise Lee's child but us. We have been hoping for years to get pregnant. But because of our busy life or some other reason it just hasn't happened and as far as I can see, I'm sorry for the mother, but this has happened for a reason and this is meant to be. I'm not thrilled with the fact that this has happened, but Lee and I survived the split-up and after the last two weeks we've had away, I feel so strong about us and that this is the right thing to do. I can only imagine what Lee must have gone through to make the decision to not see his own daughter. He did that for us, and now I'm going to do this for him. He must hurt inside, not ever seeing her. I've told Sterling however, that Lee is not to be told about this. He will want to cancel the tour and I don't think he should at this point in time. Besides, this poor little girl is going to need to adjust to me and to moving from wherever she lives and to this life. She has a whole family that she doesn't even know exists. I hope," Robin gazed at each of them with a pleading look in her eyes. "that you will agree with me and support and help us get through this adjustment until Lee comes home."

Lee's mother flew from her chair and hugged Robin so hard she had to pull away to get a breath. Jack stood up and came to Robin and hugged her as well.

"Well Sterling, it looks like our little lady here has made up her mind."

Jack began to chuckle. "And I somehow have a feeling she's going to get what she wants." Robin hugged Jack back and said,

"Thank-you."

Chapter Twenty-Five

So the arrangements were made, and as Sterling was Lee's Power of Attorney, his was the only signature needed to sign the papers. They were sent via courier that same evening and Val agreed to go with Robin to Tulsa to pick up 'Leesa Jennifer' first thing in the morning. Sterling would be traveling with them to make sure that everything went smoothly and Jack offered to get a bedroom set up for his new Granddaughter. Robin called her parents and they came over and were updated on the news. They offered to help Jack with the bedroom and getting things ready at home. Robin made them all promise not to say a word to anyone else until they worked out all the details.

After everyone had left, Robin sat in the kitchen nibbling on the vegetables that were for the dinner that never did get finished. She was so wound up. She went upstairs, but knew she wouldn't be able to sleep so she went through each of the guest bedrooms and decided to pick the one closest to theirs. She stripped the linen off the bed and made a list of what would be needed. New sheets, new pillows, maybe the room should be painted, but what color? Maybe nothing should be done until the child gets here so she can pick her own favorite colors.

"Oh, I never had any idea that this was going to be what staying at home would be like! What if I had of gone with Lee? Would any of this have happened? What would Lee have done if I didn't have to be told? What decision would he have made? I guess I won't find out for three months."

Robin sat on the bed for hours just thinking. She wondered what kind of a mother she was going to be, she wondered if this child would accept her, she prayed that she would, she prayed that everything would be all right.

Robin awoke to the telephone ringing. She went to grab it and realized that she was still fully dressed and had fallen asleep in the spare bedroom. She got up and ran to the phone in her bedroom. She glanced at the clock, it was four a.m. It was Val saying that she would be there in ten minutes, Sterling was able to book a private plane for five a.m., so they had to get going. Robin said she needed fifteen minutes. She jumped in the shower, dried off, grabbed her make-up bag, pulled her hair into a ponytail and stopped in her closet. What should she wear? She didn't want to look prim, but she didn't want to look too casual. What does a person wear when they are about to become a new mother? She settled on a long pretty flowered casual dress and cowboy boots. She grabbed a jean jacket and her bag and ran down the stairs. Her stomach was doing flips. She grabbed a banana and a bottle of water and went out the back door. Val was waiting in her Cadillac and off they went.

When the women arrived at the airport, Sterling was already waiting. They boarded and the flight left right on time. After they were underway, Sterling pulled the manila folder out of his briefcase and asked the women if they would like to see what Leesa looked like. They looked at each other and both nodded in agreement. Val gasped when she saw the baby pictures of Leesa.

"Oh my God. Look at her! She looks just like Lee as a baby. Look at that smile, it's just like Lee's."

Robin didn't know what Lee looked like as a baby of course, but she could see that unmistakable smile. There was no doubt this was his child. Then Sterling showed them the most recent photos. Her hair was very blonde with a slight curl and it was long, past her shoulders and pulled back off her face. She had dark eyes and Robin assumed they were the same dark blue as Lee's. And there it was again, that smile, complete with dimples and a grin that said, 'Hello I'm a friendly person.' She had just turned five Sterling told them and would be starting kindergarten next year. She had been enrolled in a pre-school daycare program while her mother was at work. He had no idea of what her interests were or any other information about her.

They arrived in Tulsa close to six-thirty. It would be another hour's drive to get to where Leesa was living with her mother's friends. The trio decided to stop for breakfast. Robin said she wasn't terribly hungry so they chose a Denny's to stop at. They ordered coffee and after Robin had drank half a cup, she excused herself, saying she felt nauseous. She went to the bathroom and threw-up. After five minutes and she hadn't come back out, Val went to look for her. She found Robin leaning against the sink.

"Are you okay dear?" Val asked.

Robin looked up at her, "Val do you think I'm doing the right thing?"

"Absolutely without a doubt!"

"I've never made a decision this big without Lee before. This is going to change our whole life and I didn't even discuss it with him."

"Robin, there comes a time in every wife's life that she has to decide for herself what is right and what is wrong. It could be as simple as deciding on the color to paint your bathroom to something as big as this. A good marriage consists of compromise and trust. You each have to have enough trust in each other that any decision made together or apart will be for the greater good of your marriage together. Not just deciding because that's the way you want it, but a decision based on faith and trust. I know that this is the right decision. Lee will deal with it his own way and he will probably be mad as hell that you did this without him, but in the end the decision is for the good of your marriage and your new family." She paused and pushed some stray hairs off of Robin's face and tucked them behind her ears. "Feel any better?"

"Yes, a little."

"When did you eat last?"

"I'm not sure."

"Well let's go get some food in you and go and get that new daughter, and my granddaughter!"

"Thanks Val." They both hugged.

Robin washed her face and hands and went back and ate some scrambled eggs and toast. It was just after eight a.m. by the time they got back on the road. They got lost and missed a turn off, but they eventually found the house. It was a plain little house just on the edge of town. Sterling went to the front door and Robin and Val stood beside the car and waited. A man about the same age as Sterling answered the door and he gestured for the women to come in. When they went in he introduced himself as James Allen, Jennifer's lawyer. Leesa was nowhere to be seen. Robin got a little panicked, thinking perhaps something had gone wrong, but it turned out she was upstairs crying. She didn't want to leave and go with these strange people. James explained that Leesa was very upset and didn't fully understand where she was going. After all, as long as she had been alive she didn't have a Daddy around. All she had known of her father was from some pictures of him that her mother had cut out of celebrity magazines. And what songs he sang on the radio. So to be going to see him now was scary. Robin felt sick again, but she held it back. She felt for this poor child, and asked if they could meet her.

James went upstairs and came down with a woman about the same age as Robin. She shook Robin's hand and introduced herself as Sandy. Hiding behind her was the prettiest little girl. Robin smiled at her and bent down to say hello. At that moment Robin wished she had thought to bring along a stuffed animal or some kind of a gift to give her. Leesa only hid further behind Sandy.

"Come on out sweetheart, this lady over here is your Grandmother." Sandy was saying as she tried to get Leesa's hand and pull her out from behind her. Finally she bent over and picked Leesa up. Leesa hid her face behind her hands.

"Leesa, these people are your family, they are going to take you on a plane ride to your new home."

"Nooooo! I don't want to go, I want my mommy."

Robin's eyes filled with tears. She walked over to Sandy and Leesa.

"Hello Leesa. My name is Robin and I am happy to meet you. I hope you will like living with us. We live in Texas, and we have a big house with a pool and lots of horses. You have one Grandma here, but at home you have another Grandma and two Grandpas waiting to meet you. They are back at the house trying to decide what color to paint your room and I think that we had better hurry and get back before they choose the wrong color, what do you think?"

Leesa looked at Sandy and then at Robin.

"Is my Daddy there? My Mommy told me his name was Lee, almost like mine. And he can sing real good, I know, cause we used to listen to him on the radio. Mommy said that he was famous just like I will be one day, and that's why he could never be with us. He's too busy."

Robin's eyes filled with tears again.

"Well, he is very busy. But before long he will have lots of time, and I bet he won't want to be away from you for long times ever again. But if he does have to go away, I will be with you and so will Grandma Val here. She is your Daddy's Momma. She has been waiting a long time to meet you. Do you feel ready to come with us now?"

"Uh huh. Can I bring all my stuff with me?"

Robin looked at Sandy and then at James.

"How much stuff do you have? We can take what will fit in

the car and on the plane. And then we can get the rest sent to you at your new house. How does that sound?"

"Good I guess." Leesa replied, shrugging her shoulders and playing with her hands.

"There are some things of her mother's that I think she should have. Could we send them for you to store for her until she is old enough to decide for herself what she would like to keep?" Sandy asked.

"Of course. Send whatever you like. We have plenty of room. Sterling would you make the arrangements please?" Robin asked. He nodded his head and made a note on the pad he was carrying.

"Well, if everything is in order here, I think we should be on our way."

They gathered up the things of Leesa's that were not packed up and went to the car. They said their good-byes to Sandy and thanked her for everything she had done. Robin promised they would keep in touch and anytime that they wanted to come to see Leesa or talk to her they were more than welcome. Sandy gave Leesa a huge hug and helped load the four boxes of toys and books and clothes into the trunk of the car. She handed Robin a carry-on bag.

"This is the important stuff, don't go anywhere without it. Her blanky, her favorite book and her two favorite stuffed animals, and a picture of her mother that she needs to have with her all the time. She doesn't really understand, I don't think, that her mom is gone. I am so sorry I couldn't keep Leesa with us, she is a very bright, happy, pleasant little girl. But I am happy that her father is going to be in her life now. Jennifer made a promise that she would never involve him in Leesa's life, which I never have agreed with, but, now he has no choice. I hope he will love her as much as her mother did. I don't know all the details of who he really is, other than like Leesa said, he is famous. Jennifer never did discuss him, other than it was not planned, he was married and he did take good care of them."

"I hope that you will please keep this as private as possible for now. He is out of town for awhile and until he gets back, I cannot tell him. After he has had time to adjust to her being with us, I'm sure he would love to talk to you. I will make sure that Sterling sets up a time that you could perhaps come to our home and see Leesa and meet her father. You will like him. He is a wonderful man. I think he will be very angry with himself for not getting to know his daughter. He made a mistake, which cost him our marriage for a short time. But we both knew that no matter what, we belonged together and I think that he chose me over Leesa, which had I of known she even existed, I would have insisted that he be in her life somehow, someway."

The others were all loaded in the car waiting for Robin and Sandy to finish their conversation and Leesa began banging on the window asking if they could go now.

Sandy shook Robin's hand and then hugged her and said,

"God Bless you Robin. Thank-you."

And they were on their way.

Chapter Twenty-Six

Everything went smoothly for the trip home. Robin was glad. This was Leesa's first time on a plane, so she was very excited. It was close to four p.m. when they arrived at the ranch. When they went in the back door all the other grandparents were waiting to meet Leesa. She got smothered in hugs and kisses and new toys. They had gone shopping and like any new grandparent's got carried away. They couldn't wait to show Leesa her room. They decided against painting it. It was already an ivory color so they had bought animal print sheets and comforters and filled the room with stuffed animals and books and toys. Leesa didn't know what to do first. She was lost in all the excitement and that made Robin happy. At least she wasn't sad.

They were all laughing and playing with the toys when Robin heard the phone ringing, she knew it would be Lee. They all looked at each other and Robin made a "shhh" gesture as she closed the door and went to get the phone. She ran down to the office and closed the door hoping he couldn't hear any of the frivolity going on in Leesa's bedroom.

"Hello," rushed out of her mouth before she could slow down.

"Where did I catch you?" Lee's voice asked from the other end of the phone.

"Hi Sweetheart." Robin replied calming down her tone a little. "I didn't think I was going to make it and I thought it would be you, so I ran."

"Well, how was your first day home alone?"

Oh if he only knew, Robin thought to herself.

"Well actually I spent most of the day returning phone calls. Do you know that we didn't check the machine when we got home, so I had twenty-seven messages on the machine?"

"Anything important?"

"Well a couple of things. But I can deal with them. Your doctor and dentist, that kind of stuff. You also didn't leave me an itinerary. I don't know where you are!"

Lee started laughing.

"What's so funny?" Robin asked.

"All the wives said the same thing. Ben was rushed, and we didn't have a chance to connect to check everything over before we left, but he has them all done and they are ready now. Actually if you check the fax machine it should be there, he said he would fax them right away. So, do you miss me? What else did you do today?"

Robin didn't want to lie any more than she absolutely had to, so she chose her words carefully.

"Of course I miss you. I didn't sleep well last night, but I'm hoping it will get better. Pam and Marty had a little girl just after we left Victoria and if everything goes well, they are going to come and spend Thanksgiving with us.... I mean me." Robin felt her face go red. This was going to be difficult to keep up for three months. "How was your show last night?"

"We didn't have a show last night, we drove all night. Our first show is tonight. We just finished the sound check and we're going to get some dinner and then we're on at eight tonight."

"I don't have too much else to tell you. Both of our parents hung around for awhile today. I guess they thought I needed some company. I might go shopping tomorrow or just hang around here. I haven't decided yet."

"Well should I call tomorrow or the next day?"

"Are you going to be leaving your phone on so I can get you if I need you, or should we set up a time for you to call? This is weird, all these things we've never had to deal with before. Now I understand why that itinerary is so important to all the wives."

Lee was laughing again. Robin wanted to hold him and feel his arms wrapped around her right now. She could feel the strength in his laugh and she longed to be with him.

"Honey, just hearing you laugh like that makes me miss you so much."

"You can hop on a plane anytime Robin."

"Yes I can." She said back, thinking about her journey today. "But you know I'm not going to."

"I'll call you tomorrow. Do you want me to leave the phone on?"

"No. Now that I know where you are, just call me whenever you can. If I'm home I'll talk to you, if not leave me a message. Lee I do miss you. Have a great show tonight, be good! I love you."

"I love you too Darlin'. Talk to you tomorrow."

"Bye."

"Bye."

Robin hung up the phone hating herself for deceiving her husband, but at least it was a good deception, it could be worse.

Making her way back down the hall, she could hear that things had quieted down. Reaching the bedroom she saw Grandma Val sitting in a new rocking chair with Leesa snuggled in beside her reading a story and Grandma Diane laying on the bed listening to the story too. The grandpas had made their way downstairs and were having a drink and watching television.

"You know what ladies? I think it's time this young lady got ready for bed." Robin said when Val had finished the story.

"I wonder if you have any pajamas in these dressers?"

Grandma Diane got off the bed and pulled open a drawer and pulled out a new and freshly washed pretty nightie. She then showed Robin what else had been purchased. Some underwear and socks, a couple of pairs of blue jeans and two tops.

"I sure could have got carried away but I wasn't sure what size or what she needed so I thought these would do for now and you two can go shopping for anything else Leesa may need. I looked at shoes, but that is something else she needs to be with you to buy. Boy oh boy Leesa, I sure am happy you came here to live. I hope you like it here and settle in with Robin, she is a wonderful person and she will take real good care of you."

Diane went over to the rocker and kissed Leesa on the top of her head. "Goodnight little one. See you in the mornin'." She turned and gave Robin a big hug and kissed her on the cheek, and then left the room.

Val still sat in the rocker with her arm around Leesa. Robin could see in her eyes that Val was happy. Val looked up at Robin,

"Do you mind if I help her get ready for bed?"

What else could Robin say but,

"Of course not. Leesa, let's get you into these pajamas and then we can go downstairs and say goodnight and thank-you to everyone and then you and I can have a snack before bed."

Robin took Leesa's hand and helped her out of the rocking chair and between her and Val, they managed to get everything ready for bed. Leesa picked out a couple of new stuffed animals that she wanted to sleep with and then asked where her own things were. Robin found the bag that Sandy had told Robin not to lose. From inside of it they pulled out a little pink Teddy bear that Leesa said was her best friend and her name was Lucy. Then she took out a stuffed giraffe whose name was Melville and a worn blanket that Leesa said was hers since the day she was born. Robin and Val looked at each other, both feeling the sudden sadness that filled the room. Then they pulled out a photograph in a golden frame. It was obviously Jennifer. She and Leesa were sitting on a swing set. Robin froze. This woman was beautiful. She could see why Lee had been attracted to her. And she could now see that Leesa did very much look like her father. Leesa watched the two women looking silently at the photograph.

"That's me and my Mommy at Bishop's park. We used to go there all the time." She said in a slow small voice.

"Where would you like to put this picture Leesa?" Robin asked. "Would you like it on your night table here so you can see it when you go to sleep and wake up?"

"It might make me sad to see it there." Leesa replied looking up at Robin.

"Oh sweetie," Robin held Leesa, "I don't want you to be sad. I just thought you might miss your Mommy and want to have her picture close to you."

Leesa began to cry. "I do miss my Mommy, I want her to come back."

Val decided to quietly leave the room and let Robin deal with this alone. She knew that it wasn't going to be easy, but Robin had to do it. Val knew she could.

Robin held Leesa for a long time and just let her cry. She didn't know quite what else to do. When the tears slowed down Robin began to talk.

"You know Leesa, I'm not your Mama and I don't want you to ever think that I can replace her. But I do want to be your friend and your Daddy and I want to give you a nice home and when you get to meet him and he is here more often I think we will all be happy. I know this is all real hard right now, but we have to try. And if you feel sad I will understand. And if you want to cry or if you miss your Mama, that's o.k. too. I will be here for you Leesa. You can come to me no matter what kind of trouble or feelings you have. Okay?"

Leesa hugged Robin and said, "I'm hungry!"

Robin started laughing and stood up and took Leesa's hand.

"Come on then, let's go find something to eat.

They went downstairs and found a note saying goodnight from the new Grandparents. They would call in the morning.

Robin made toast with jam and poured two glasses of milk. She and Leesa sat in the kitchen and ate. They made some small talk. Robin asked Leesa what she liked to eat and told her that she was a chef and could cook almost anything. Leesa said her favorite food was pizza.

It was going on ten o'clock, so Robin said it was time they got to bed. She gave Leesa another tour of the house and when they stopped at Robin's bedroom she asked Leesa to sit on the bed while she got her pajamas on. Robin went into the bathroom and washed her face and brushed her teeth and got changed. When she came out brushing her hair, she found Leesa lying on the bed fast asleep; holding onto a photo of Lee that had been on Robin's night table. Robin took the photo carefully out of Leesa's hands and gently lifted her and carried her to her new bedroom. When she returned to her own room, she picked up the picture of Lee and was about to return it to its place on her night table. But, changing her mind, she took it to Leesa's room and placed it on her night table so she would see it when she woke up.

Chapter Twenty-Seven

Robin had a restless sleep. She kept listening for Leesa to call out or cry or wake up scared, but she didn't. Finally in the early morning hours Robin drifted into sleep and was suddenly awoken by the motion of the bed moving. Quickly awakening, Robin dizzily sat up only to find that Leesa had climbed into the bed beside her. Without startling her, Robin said, "Good morning Leesa. How did you sleep?"

"Fine thank-you. Can I cuddle with you? Mommy and me used to cuddle every morning before she had to go to work."

"I would be pleased to cuddle with you." Robin wrapped her arm around Leesa and the two of them snuggled under the covers with Lucy the Teddy and the worn blanket.

"Well what do you think we should do today? I don't have to go to work, so we can spend all day together."

"I dunno." Leesa replied staring at Robin.

"Well, we can go shopping, or I can introduce you to all the horses and show you the ranch……"

"How come you don't have to go to work?" Leesa interrupted.

"Well I don't have a job anymore so I stay home. Actually

I usually travel with your Daddy, but I stayed home this trip so I could do some work around the house and get ready for Thanksgiving and Christmas and, well, to do things here."

"Hmm. How do you get money if you don't work? My Mommy had to go to work to get money so we could buy stuff."

"Well honey, your Daddy makes enough money to take care of all of us."

"Me too?"

"Yes you too!"

"That's good. I'm hungry."

"Good, lets go and get some breakfast and I know we are definitely going to have to go grocery shopping because I'm sure you won't enjoy yogurt and vegetables for the next three months."

"Yuck!"

"That's what I thought!" Robin laughed and pulled back the covers and climbed out of bed. She went into her bathroom and Leesa followed her. They washed their faces and hands and brushed their hair. Robin dressed in a pair of pink sweat pants, T-shirt and slippers. Then they went to Leesa's room and dressed her in a pair of new blue jeans and a T-shirt. Holding hands they went downstairs to the kitchen. Robin made them scrambled eggs and toast, only because that was all she had. Robin went through the cupboards making notes of things she would need to pick up. After the dishes were cleaned up, Robin asked Leesa to play in her room while she had a shower and got ready so they could go out. While in the shower, Robin panicked. What if she falls while I'm in here? What if she hurts herself and I don't hear her. She didn't waste any time. She was in and out, calling for Leesa as soon as she shut off the water. The child didn't answer so Robin grabbed a bathrobe and ran to Leesa's room. There she was lying on her stomach reading a book.

"Hey Leesa, are you okay?" Robin tried to calm her voice.

"Yes, I'm fine. I like this book."

"Good, good, you keep looking at it and I'll finish getting ready." Robin walked back to her own room heaving a heavy sigh and thinking to herself that this was really going to take some getting used to. As she was dressing the phone rang. It was her Mom asking how the night went. Robin briefly explained, not wanting to leave Leesa alone for too long. Robin asked her mother to come shopping with them. She thought that having someone else along might help until she got used to watching out for Leesa. As soon as she hung up from that call the phone rang again. It was Val this time. The conversation was almost the same and she too was going to join them shopping.

They bought out the grocery store. At least that's how Robin felt. She bought things she had never even heard of before or paid attention to. She had to read labels and check sugar content and fats and additives. The grandmas were telling her to lighten up, even her own mother who was still a vegetarian was saying things like, "She's just a kid, let her try it." Robin was amazed how these two grown women had transformed overnight. She wasn't regretting it, just amazed at how one small child could change so many peoples' lives. She now understood a lot of the things that she had heard from Pam and Sara over the years. It was a huge responsibility. She only hoped she could do it.

"Robin, could we have lunch at that place?" Leesa asked, pointing to the fast food restaurant across the street.

This would be a first for Robin. She wasn't too thrilled with the idea, but again she gave in. After careful scrutiny of the menu, Robin decided that the food wasn't that bad after all.

When they got back to the ranch, the grandmas amused Leesa while Robin put away the groceries and began to make preparations for spaghetti dinner. She made a jug of iced tea and asked the ladies if they would like to sit out on the deck and enjoy the afternoon sun. That was the first time Leesa had seen the pool. She was so excited to go swimming. Robin didn't know if it would be warm enough, or if Leesa could swim and how much water experience she had. She thought to herself,

'Oh God, this pool is going to be a huge worry. I'm going to have to make sure to lock all the doors that come out back. And never leave her alone out here.' She watched Leesa carefully walk around the edge of the pool. Robin tuned back into the conversation that was going on around her. They were discussing whether Leesa should go in or not. Finally Leesa came to Robin and asked her,

"Can I please go for a swim? I have tooken swimming lessons since I was a baby."

"You have?"

"Yes. Please Robin, can I?"

"Well I suppose. But I didn't think about getting you a bathing suit. Do you think you might have one in your boxes of things we brought with us?"

"I used to have one when I lived at my other house." Her eyes looked down and she played with her fingers. "It was blue."

"Let's go see." Robin took her hand and they went into the house and up to the third bedroom where Robin had asked for all the boxes of Leesa's things to be taken. The first box was books and then toys and then they found the clothes. They had pulled out almost everything in the box before they found the blue bathing suit.

"Yeah!" exclaimed Leesa.

"I guess I will have to find a suit and come in with you too. Can you put this on yourself and put your clothes on your bed while I go and find my suit?"

"Yes I can." She replied politely.

Robin walked Leesa to her room and then went to her own to change into her bathing suit. She pulled her hair into a pony-tail and then into a bun. Then she went to the linen closet in the laundry room to get them each a towel. When they were ready to go downstairs, Robin asked Leesa if she remembered to go to the bathroom.

"Whoops! I forgot." And she ran back to the bathroom in her bedroom. Robin followed her into the bedroom and when she was finished in the bathroom, pulled Leesa's hair into a bun as well.

"Alright, I think we are ready to go now." Robin handed Leesa a towel and they went down the stairs and out to the pool.

The grandmas were sitting talking and showed delight when Leesa walked past in her little blue bathing suit with a cut-out on the tummy. She put her towel down on one of the lounge chairs and then proceeded to the stairs of the pool. Robin followed right behind her not wanting Leesa to get too far ahead just in case she couldn't swim. But it turned out she in fact could. She walked right down the steps and jumped in and came up doing the front crawl. Robin asked her not to go past the center of the pool unless she was with her and Leesa didn't. Leesa showed them everything that she had learned in swimming lessons. After Robin felt confident that Leesa was safe in the water, she relaxed a bit and they both had fun. Leesa would have stayed in all afternoon, Robin was sure. But it was getting close to dinner and Robin still wanted to show Leesa the horses. The grandmas left them alone floating on air mattresses that Robin found in the pool shed. Not long after the grandmas had left, the girls got out of the pool and dried off. They sat outside for awhile and then Robin said,

"Let's go get out of these wet suits and into some dry clothes so we can go and get dinner started.

"Can we go swimming again?" Leesa asked.

"Not today. But we can go tomorrow if you like. And Leesa I'm sure you know, but I just want to be sure that you never play out here alone or go near the water unless someone else is with you. Do you understand?"

"Yes, I know that." Leesa replied, looking up at Robin.

"Well I thought you would, but we haven't ever had any children in this house so I'm not sure how child proof and how safe it is. For now, until we can figure out how safe everything is and until you know your way around here, I need you to stay close to me or your grandparents when you're outside. Alright?"

"Okay. Robin, I'm really hungry."

Robin laughed. She couldn't believe how much this little girl could eat. She was sure that she ate more than Robin did in a day. They went upstairs to change. Robin turned on the television in her room for Leesa to watch while she got changed. Before they went downstairs, Robin went to the office to check the answering machine. Four calls. She played them back just to see if Lee had called. None of the messages where from him.

" Thank God I didn't miss him." Robin thought to herself. I don't know what I will tell him happened today. Perhaps the truth? Your mother, my mother and me, we just sat around the pool drinking iced tea. Sure that was all he needed to hear.

Dinner was cooked and Leesa and Robin were sitting at the island in the kitchen eating. It was almost six o'clock. They were chatting about clothes and Robin was asking Leesa if she would like to go shopping and get anything new. Leesa wasn't sure, but she didn't think so. After the dinner dishes were all cleaned up, Robin took Leesa out to the barn and introduced her to the horses. Leesa was so excited.

"I didn't really think that you would have horses this close to your house and that we could come and see them whenever we wanted and that you had so many!" She exclaimed!

"Robin, can we go for a ride? Please!" She was almost begging.

Robin was patting Ginger as she turned to Leesa and said, "Not tonight Sweetie. It's too late, the horses are all put into their stalls for the night. Maybe tomorrow." She walked over to Leesa who was looking a tad disappointed. "Don't worry Leesa, you live here now. We can do this stuff everyday. If we have enough time."

"Can we really?"

"Mm hmm, we sure can!"

"We couldn't do any of this where I used to live. We had to drive to the pool and it was the community pool so there was always lots of people there. And we never had any horses. Robin

I think I do need to go shopping, I think if I live here I need some cowboy boots."

"What, you don't have any cowboy boots?" Robin threw her hand to her forehead. "Oh my goodness we can't have a pretty little girl living on a ranch in Texas with no cowboy boots. Our first order of duty tomorrow will be to get into town and order you some spiffy new cowboy boots. Right now though, we had better get you into bed."

Holding hands they walked into the house. When Leesa was all ready for bed and Robin was about to sit and read to her, the phone rang. Robin quickly said, "You stay in bed, I'll be right back."

She ran down the hall to the office so Leesa wouldn't hear the conversation.

"Hello." She said in the calmest voice she could manage.

"Hi Darlin'. Miss me yet?"

"Hi Lee. Yes, I missed you even before you left. You know that."

"I know. I just like to tease you. What's new today?"

"Not much. Just hung around the pool with our Mom's. I took it easy today. I have to go to town tomorrow, so I was just lazy."

"Are you feeling alright? It's not like you to sit around and do nothing."

"I'm fine. I guess the Mom's just like having me home so they are hanging around. I don't know. Maybe they think I'm lonely. Hopefully it will wear off in a day or two because I have a lot of things I really want to do around here."

"It doesn't sound like you're lonely yet, so I guess I'll just keep working until you are!"

Robin could hear the smile is his voice and she missed seeing it on his face.

"How's it going so far?"

"Great. The crowd last night was really pumped. We haven't been here for a long time so they were ready to see the new show.

It was good. Nothing exciting to report, business as usual. Well, we're just getting into our show clothes so I'll let you go and talk to you tomorrow. Sleep well Rob, talk to you tomorrow. Love ya!"

"I love you too."

"Bye."

"Bye."

Robin hung up the phone and ran back to Leesa's bedroom only to find her sound asleep. She put the book that she was going to read back on the shelf, gently kissed Leesa on the forehead, turned out the light and left the room.

'How on earth am I going to keep this up for three months?' She thought to herself as she went downstairs. She decided that it had been another long day and she was exhausted so she would go to bed too. She locked up the house, turned out the lights, hit the security alarm and went to bed. It was a quarter past eight.

Chapter Twenty-Eight

The next few weeks were filled with Robin and Leesa getting to know and adjust to each other. Robin was learning a lot about children very quickly and Leesa was in heaven every day finding new things to see and do. Robin left Leesa with her Grandparents when she went to town to do business and check on the Honky-Tonk. She managed to keep up the charade with Lee. He wasn't calling every day now so it was easy to leave out some things when they talked. But, it also made Robin feel sad that she couldn't share all of this with Lee and he was missing out on all the new discoveries that both Leesa and herself were making. But then she also thought how he would have his own time to spend with Leesa by himself and he and she would be able to form their own bond when he came home.

One day in early October, Robin had gone into town to pay bills and to do business at the bar. She had left Leesa with Grandpa Jack as he was getting some new 'baby cows' that he had bought at the auction on the weekend and she wanted to see them. Jack said he would love the company. He was thrilled to have Leesa here to share all of the things that were everyday to him, but new to her.

When Robin came home, had parked the Porsche and was unloading her purchase's, Val came walking into the garage to find her.

"Robin?"

"Hi Val. How's everything?"

"Well, Leesa has had a little accident."

"Oh God!" Robin dropped the packages she was holding and grabbed one of Val's arms. "Is she alright? What happened?"

"She's fine. She fell in the barn on the edge of the cement floor and hurt her arm. She let out a few good yelps and…." Val smiled, "scared the hell out of Grandpa Jack. He's sitting inside with her. We wrapped it and put some cold compresses on it. But I think you should get it looked at. I didn't know if you had a doctor for her yet or if she would go to yours. Anyway we comforted her as best we could and told her you would be home soon."

"Oh Val, I'm sorry I wasn't here for you and for her."

"She asked for you a couple of times. We told her you wouldn't be long. You better get in and see her."

Val picked up the parcels Robin had dropped as Robin ran into the house. She found Leesa and Jack curled up on one of the big couches watching television. Robin went right to Leesa and knelt down and gave her a big hug.

"Hey Sweetie. I hear you had a little fall." Leesa looked up at Robin with tears in her eyes. She didn't speak she just nodded her head.

"Hi Jack." Robin glanced over at him. He had a look of concern on his face.

"I think she is going to be fine Robin. Probably badly bruised. She was running and slipped just at the doorway and fell on top of her arm, right on the edge of the cement."

"Can I look at it Leesa?" Robin asked.

"It really hurts." Leesa replied.

"Do you think we should go see a doctor?"

"Yes. I think it's broken." And Leesa burst into tears.

Jack stood up and said,

"I think you'd better take her, just for her own piece of mind, if nothing else."

"Leesa, you just sit here with Grandpa Jack for a minute and I'll go call my doctor and tell him we're coming. I'll be right back."

When Robin came back she had picked up a sweater for Leesa and said,

"Let's go. Dr. Mike is waiting for us."

Mike Robertson was a great doctor. He was about the same age as Lee and Robin, and he would drop anything for them. He knew their lives were busy and when they were in need of his services he made himself available. Robin had talked to the receptionist and said who she was and what had happened. The girl said she would get them in as soon as they got there. Val offered to go with them. They went in the Explorer and Val sat in the backseat with Leesa as Robin drove.

The twenty-minute drive to the office went well. Leesa winced every time she moved her arm, but she didn't cry. When they arrived at the office the receptionist wasn't too sure what to do as Robin did not have any medical records for Leesa and she wasn't a registered patient. As Robin was trying to explain, Mike came out. He said to the receptionist,

"Don't worry about that right now. Give me Mrs. Cotton's file and let me see the patient."

She then led Robin and Leesa into the examining room, Val said she would wait in the reception area.

"Who is this beautiful young lady you have with you today Mrs. Cotton?" Mike asked as he lifted Leesa onto the examining table.

"Well Dr. Mike, it's a long story, but this is Lee's daughter, Leesa."

He looked at Robin and then at Leesa without any expression on his face.

"I can sure see that now. You sure do look like your Daddy." Mike smiled at Leesa.

"Do you know my Daddy?" She asked looking up at Mike with big questioning eyes.

"I sure do. I'm his doctor. Why don't you tell me what happened to your arm Leesa."

She told the story with much more enthusiasm than Jack had. And Mike paid direct attention to each detail and every pain she told about. When she finished the story he took off the wrap, cleaned up the scrape and pushed and moved her arm and each finger and made her wiggle them in front of her nose. She laughed but said it hurt a little. He assured her that it wasn't broken and in a couple of days she would probably have a big bruise but her arm would be as good as new in no time. When he was done he offered her a red lollipop and asked if he could speak with Robin alone.

"Honey, can you go and sit with Grandma Val for a few minutes while I talk with Dr. Mike?"

"Okay."

Robin took Leesa out to Val who offered to take her for a walk outside.

When Robin returned to the examining room Mike asked,

"What's going on Robin? This is big news and you haven't even informed me."

Robin filled Mike in on the whole story of how Leesa had come to be with her, where Lee was right now and that he didn't even know that she had come to live with them yet.

"Wow. You have taken on a big responsibility Robin. Are you prepared for this?"

"No." She replied honestly. "I had no idea how much…." She was lost for words. "not work, not responsibility, but how emotionally draining this is. Don't get me wrong, I'm starting to love her. Actually I fell in love with her the moment I saw her and saw how much she looked like Lee. But my entire life is different now and it's all so new to me. But, the hardest part is keeping it from Lee."

"Why don't you tell him?"

"He's on a three month tour and it would be too much to reschedule now. Plus when I found out I thought that it would be great for her and I to get to know each other alone and then when he gets home he will have her to himself, without trying to get to know the both of us at the same time. But Mike, if you can help me and give me any advice, I sure can use it. See, I haven't told anyone other than family yet because you know the press. If they get a hold of this it will be world news before Lee even knows. I've told a few people she is Lee's niece. That's easy, but I can't say that in front of Leesa. I don't want to hurt her feelings or make her think I don't want to admit who she really is. I'm afraid I'm going to scar her for life and she will hate me if I don't watch what I say."

"Does she call you Mom?"

"No I told her to call me Robin. She seems to be fine with that."

"Does she ever ask for her Mother?"

"Yes. Sometimes at night. I try to comfort her and we talk about her Mom. I think she can almost accept that her Mom is gone, but she doesn't understand where her Dad is."

"What have you told her?"

"That he is away working and will be home soon."

"Good. I was going to recommend that she be around other children, like in pre-school or some other activity where she will be with other kids. If she was used to being in a daycare everyday, she might think she is on like a vacation now. You have to get her into a routine of sorts so she will know that this is her life. Is her last name the same as yours?"

"No it is her Mother's name. But when Lee gets home I would like to change it."

"Is there anyone else who could drop her off and pick her up from school? Like a grandparent or a friend? Actually forget I said that. That idea wouldn't work either. She would wonder why you weren't doing it. Let's think. When does Lee get home?"

"In December, just before Christmas. Why?"

"That will work. You and her will have this time together and then when Lee gets home and the word gets out, so to say, she can go to school then. I think it might be hard for both of them then, but she needs some continuity in her life. And being a part of your life is going to be a major change for her don't forget."

"I know already. Everyday she discovers something that I just take for-granted. Like the pool and the horses, new books that don't come from the library. I know it must be a huge change for her, but I'm trying my best to not overwhelm her."

"That's good and you know I will help you. If there is ever anything that you're concerned about, anything Robin, just give me a call." He looked her in the eye and patted her on the hand. "And I believe that you are well overdue yourself for and exam. I think that if you don't mind we should do it while you're here because you've got your hands full and I can see you look exhausted. Here get changed into this gown and we will do a complete physical."

He handed Robin a pink paper dressing gown and left the room. When he came back a few minutes later he said,

"I told your Mother-in-law that while I had you here I was going to do your physical. She said that Leesa and her hadn't eaten lunch yet, so they were going to go to the restaurant across the street and grab a bite so I could take my time. So let's see," He opened her medical file. "you haven't had a Pap smear done in over two years, we need to do that and I think I will get some blood work updated, and just a general check." He looked up from the file. "I will need some information. Date of your last period?" He looked over at Robin who was sitting on the examining table playing with the paper gown.

"I don't know. I haven't thought about it lately. We've been so busy that I can't remember. Let me think. We went to Victoria the beginning of September, I must have had it since then. I'd have to look on my calendar at home. Sorry."

"I sure don't envy your life. I don't know how you can keep track of everything."

"You know Mike, since Leesa has come into it I can't even remember what I did before she came. We do have an extremely busy life. But none of it compares to the moments I just sit and look at life through her eyes. It's amazing what we don't see as adults and it's amazing the things we're missing out on."

Mike began to laugh. "I love it when people have children. Remember, I have three and with each of them I've seen life differently. Lay down, let's get this over with so you can join your family for lunch."

Robin shifted the gown and lay on her back as Mike pulled her legs down and put her feet into the stirrups. He then got the instruments ready and turned on the light. He put on the latex gloves and began the exam. He felt around her belly and abdomen.

"Do you think you could be due for your period soon?" He asked as he continued feeling her belly.

"I honestly don't know, but I must be because it seems like it's been a while since I've had one."

He was about to do the internal and had spread her legs apart, but stopped what he was doing.

"Robin, is there any chance that you could be pregnant?"

She sat up. "Why?"

"Well, I feel something inside and the color I see down here tells me you very well could be. How do your breasts feel, are they tender?"

"Yeah, kinda."

"Have you noticed any weight gain?"

"My clothes have been feeling a little tight lately, but I just figured that since Leesa has been here I've been eating things I normally wouldn't and I haven't been getting the exercise that I usually do."

"How about your emotions. Are they out of whack?"

Robin began to laugh.

"Well considering what I've gong through the last few weeks I'm sure anyone would be out of whack. Do you really think I could be?"

"We can quickly find out." He stood up and opened a cupboard then handed Robin a specimen bottle. "Go fill this."

She wrapped the gown around her behind and went into the adjoining bathroom and filled the bottle. When she came back and handed it to Mike he asked,

"Are you going to be fine with this if you are pregnant?"

"Mike you should know that that is a stupid question to be asking me."

He put a paper swab into the specimen jar. "It will be a couple of minutes. I was just wondering, now that you have Leesa, if this would be too much all at once."

"Are you nuts? This would be so perfect, you have no idea how thrilling this would be. Just think Mike, our lives are already going to be adjusting to Leesa, this couldn't be happening at a more perfect time. Everything in life happens for a reason. I'm starting to believe that more everyday."

They both turned to look at the swab in the jar. It had turned a dark blue. Mike pulled it out of the bottle and asked,

"Do you know what this means?"

Robin shook her head, no.

"My dear, you are going to have a baby."

Robin jumped off the chair she had sat in and hugged Mike.

"Are you for sure? No errors, no mistakes, no doubts?"

"These are ninety-nine percent accurate, but just so we know for sure and how far along you are, let's get you in for an ultrasound. But let's finish this exam first."

Mike finished off the physical and gave Robin the papers to order blood work and the ultrasound. He told her he would call the lab, which was right next door, and get her in right now. She got changed back into her clothes and was waiting for him to return. So much was going through her mind she started to cry. Oh God, this explains so much. Why I was so emotional over Lee leaving, the nausea I've been feeling. And I thought it was all my nerves. I was starting to think I was going to have a nervous breakdown or something. She smiled through her tears. What a time for all this to be happening and I have to go through it alone. I can do it. I have my parents and Lee's parents who will all be here to help. And now I have Leesa. When Lee gets home, he is going to be in for the shock of his life. I'm not going to tell him about this either. He can get it all when he comes home!

Chapter Twenty-Nine

When Robin finally joined up with Val and Leesa in the restaurant,

Val was looking greatly concerned.

"Robin, what took so long?"

Robin scooted in beside Leesa in the booth and gave her a kiss on the top of her head.

"Val, you are not going to believe this," Robin looked over at Val with tears in her eyes. "I'm three months pregnant!"

Val's hands immediately covered her mouth and she began to cry tears of joy for Robin.

"Oh Robin. Congratulations. How long have you known about this?"

"I didn't have a clue Val. I've been feeling weird lately, but I just figured it was everything that was going on in my life." Leesa looked up at Robin then,

"Are you sick Robin?" She asked.

Robin wrapped her arm around Leesa and stroked her hair.

"Oh no Honey, no, not at all. It looks like you are going to have a baby brother or sister to add to this new family you've got."

"Why are you crying then?" She looked puzzled.

"We are just very happy. Your Daddy and I have wanted to have children for a long time, but it never happened. You must be our good luck charm, 'cause now we have you and we are going to have another baby too."

"Are you going to tell Lee about this?" Val asked.

"I don't think so. I think considering all that's happened so far let's just add this to the list and save it till he gets home. Besides I want to see his face when he sees me." Quickly calculating she added, "I'll be five months when he comes home. I should be showing by then. I don't know how I'm going to keep all the other girls from telling the other guys though. I think I need to have them all over for dinner and tell them everything and to make sure they all keep it from Lee. Let's go home, I can't wait to tell Jack and my parents."

When Robin got home she shared her news with her family who were just as thrilled as she was. She sat down with a calendar and tried to decide when to have the dinner party with the wives. She picked Halloween. They could all bring their kids and it could be a fun party. Not only to share this news, but to introduce Leesa as well.

So, over the next few weeks, plans were made and party goods filled the house. Robin had planned many parties before, but none ever for children. Again she was fascinated with this event through the eyes of a child. She had sent out invitations to each child individually asking them to arrive in costumes with their Mom's. There would be prizes for the best costumes and games and of course lots of food. Robin had fun going through party books and finding Halloween recipes.

Leesa decided she wanted to be a cowgirl. Robin tried to talk her into something else because a cowgirl in Texas was the norm. But Leesa insisted. So they both dressed the same. Robin had bought Leesa a new pair of white with blue inlaid leather cowboy boots. Robin had her own blue pair, so they dressed up in skirts with sequins and big silver belt buckles and pretty satin blouses with sequin designs all over, and white cowboy hats to top off the outfits. Robin's pregnancy was starting to show, so she wore her blouse un-tucked, and had the belt slung low on her waist. It would be obvious to anyone who knew her, that she was pregnant.

As soon as the guests began to arrive, the news was out. As each family arrived and noticed Robin, she was hugged and there were tears. After everyone had arrived the kids were sent to the 'party room'. Robin had hired some help for the evening so she could enjoy the party too. She had also hired a children's entertainer to put on a show for them. After the Mom's all got the kids under control, they left them and went into the family room. Robin had them all gather around so she could tell them her news.

With as little detail as possible, she explained what had happened with Jennifer and how Leesa had come to be with her as well as the news of her pregnancy.

"So y'all see what I've been doing since the guys left town. I'm so sorry that I haven't had time to let you know sooner about any of this," she patted her belly and everyone started to laugh, "it was a total surprise to me too. But I need to ask you all as my closest and dearest friends, to please keep this as much a secret as possible. I just don't want Lee to find out yet. You know him, he will want to come home and this tour was too important to them to cancel any dates. Even if they get a couple of days off he could come home, but I don't want him to yet. He was planning to do some writing and he needs his time alone to do that. And quite frankly, I need time to adjust to having a five-year-old around, and getting ready for a baby. I want to be comfortable with all this myself and have everything ready when he gets home so that he and Leesa will get to spend as much time together as they can. They have so much to learn about each other."

"Robin, how are you holding up after finding out about Leesa?" Becky asked, "I'm not sure I would want a child that was someone else's! Especially under the circumstances."

The words were harsh and sarcastic, not like Becky. Robin was confused about the sarcasm in her friend's comment.

"Well Becky. When Sterling first told me I was shocked of course. But I already knew about the affair, y'all did too." She glanced around at the faces all listening intently. They were all thinking back to the months that Lee and Robin were apart several years ago. Each remembering in their own way how they had helped both Lee and Robin through it. They all nodded. "After Sterling explained that the mother had no family for Leesa to go to and when he told me that Lee had never even seen her, I realized that this was his child too. He was her father whether he acknowledged it or not, she belongs with him, with us. Not in a foster home or adopted to just anyone. Once I saw her and saw how much she looked like him, I knew deep in my heart that I had done the right thing."

"Robin, what has happened to you?" Virginia asked.

"What do you mean?" Robin questioned.

Virginia got up and moved beside where Robin was sitting and leaned over and gave her a big hug.

"I don't mean anything bad. I am so proud that you had the courage to forgive Lee and accept his child into your home. I know," she pulled back from Robin and looked her straight in the eyes, "that you had a rough time getting over 'The Affair' and we all know that is why you started travelling with the band all the time." Virginia glanced around at all the other women who were all nodding in agreement with her.

Robin looked down at her hands that she had folded in her lap.

"You didn't want it to happen again." Virginia stood up and began walking around the room. "And, hell, between all of us, who knows how many 'affairs' have gone on over the years." She looked up at the ceiling to avoid eye contact with anyone in particular. "And not just with the guys! We can't judge what is right or wrong to you, only you can. All of us are in this business together. We don't lead a regular life here girls. Our husbands have too many choices and we either have to accept them for who and what they are, no matter what, and hope they love us enough to wait till they get home, or, we live with the consequences. I have chosen to live with the consequences. Billy loves me, and the kids, I know that. I love the fame and money and things that his job has given us. But it's his choice. Whatever choices he makes, he makes and he is the one who has to live with them. I'm getting carried away here, I'm sorry. I just want you to know that I think Robin has done the right thing. And besides, the big picture is that this child needed a home and a family who will love her and what better place than with her natural father. I promise to you Robin, that I will do my best in trying to keep this a secret until Lee gets home."

All the other women started clapping and saying they would also do their best in keeping it a secret. They were all talking and laughing amongst themselves. Robin had gone into the kitchen to check on some hors d'oeuvres when she heard a knock at the back door. Before she could get to it, Jose and Maria came walking in. They had their arms full of things. They unloaded everything on the island and were giving hugs to everyone, when Jose reached Robin he hugged her tight and started crying.

"Oh my Robin. I knew you had good news to tell me. I just knew it when you called and invited us. How far along are you?" He asked as he patted her belly.

"About four months." She beamed. "But Jose, Lee hasn't been told yet. It's a secret until he gets home from the tour in December."

"In December?" He questioned. "You must tell him before then!"

"No Jose. He can just wait!" Robin was laughing. "And you can just wait too because I have another surprise for you." She glanced at her watch, "But you will have to wait about a half hour."

"What you tell me Robin! I can't wait!"

"Sure you can, come on sit down have some food and I'll get you a drink."

Maria hugged and kissed Robin on both cheeks and patted her belly very softly. "I prayed for you Robin that one day this would happen, your dreams will be filled. You and Lee will make wonderful parents. I am so happy for you both." Robin noticed a slight tearing in Maria's eyes.

Robin then led Jose and Maria into the family room and got them each a drink. Jose a glass of good red wine and Maria a soda.

Robin went back into the kitchen and put the pizzas in the oven for the kid's. She had prepared crepes ahead of time and put them in the warming oven and was stirring the fillings. She had made three choices, seafood, chicken, or spinach and feta cheese. The table was set in the dining room for everyone. One end of the table was set for the kids with paper plates that had Halloween scenes with matching napkins and cups. Robin had added to her linen collection by purchasing twenty-four assorted Halloween place mats and napkins. She used the cloth napkins for the adults, but Leesa wanted the napkins that matched the plates and cups for the kids.

Robin took the prepared endive salad out of the fridge and placed it on the table, opened two bottles of white wine, put them in wine coolers and put them on the table. She poured the fillings for the crepes into serving dishes and just when she was checking on the desserts, all the kids came running into the family room. The entertainer was finished and now it was time to eat. While the Mothers and helpers got the children's hands washed and everyone settled, Robin took Leesa and Jose and Maria aside and introduced them.

"Leesa, I would like you to meet some very, very special people." Robin said as she knelt down and put her arm on Leesa's shoulder. "This is Jose and this is Maria."

Leesa waved shyly and said, "Hello."

"They are very good friends of your Daddy's and mine."

Jose's hand flew to his chest.

"My God Robin, who is this lovely young lady, is she your daughter? Did you have a child you didn't tell us about?"

Robin was laughing.

"Run off and join the others at the table Honey."

"Okay. Bye." Leesa waved and off she went to join her new friends.

"Robin, you have too many secrets. Would you like to share with us?" Maria asked.

"You won't believe this………" Robin briefly explained the story to them and again Jose was in tears. He was hugging Robin, while Maria was wiping her eyes.

"You have too much excitement around here Robin. I am so happy for you. I told you one day you would have lots of children. Two, that's lots more than one and both at the same time. Oh Robin this makes me so happy. I only hope that Lee will be as happy. He is a very lucky man!"

Chapter Thirty

The next event that kept Robin busy was having Pam and Marty come to stay for two weeks during Thanksgiving.

They arrived the week before and Robin had kept all her secrets to herself until they arrived. Needless to say, they had a lot to talk about. Robin was having both sets of parents, as well as both her and Lee's brothers and their wives for Christmas dinner, so Thanksgiving was just their parents, and whatever ranch hands were kicking around with no place to go as well as Pam and Marty. Robin had tried to prepare as much as she could ahead of time.

She was doing a good job of keeping tabs on things at the Honky-Tonk, running the house, taking care of Leesa, and trying to prepare for Christmas. She was also doing a very good job of her selective conversations with Lee. He called almost every other day, unless something else was up. Like television or radio interviews and autograph sessions before and after shows. He said he had been doing a lot of writing and was pleased with his results. He was looking forward to getting home. The tour was fun, but he really missed having her along. Robin, fortunately had been so busy with all the things she was doing, that she had plenty to tell him without telling everything. It was hard to fill in the days that her and Leesa had spent at a park or just shopping, but she gave the very least information and changed the subject, quickly.

The visit with Pam and Marty went terrific. Leesa played well with Jordan and the baby was great. Pam couldn't drink as she was still nursing and of course Robin couldn't either. She really wanted to show them the Honkey-Tonk at night when there was a band playing, but she also didn't want to be seen too much around there until Lee knew the news. She took them for lunch one day and introduced Marty to Chet and asked him to make Marty comfortable when he came back. The girls would get to talking and poor Marty had nothing to do. Robin gave him the keys to her car and told him to go "paint the town" whenever he felt like it. Pam was happy that he could go off and explore when he had had enough of being the only guy with these two hormonal women. They laughed about it a lot and Marty really didn't mind going off on his own. Besides, he was driving the Porsche. Who would complain about that?

So, most nights after the kids where in bed and the girls had made their evening pot of tea, Marty would take off to the Bar. He would come home with stories and having had a great time. And Robin and Pam would have had another great night of just sitting and talking. They did a few fun things too. They all went shopping in Dallas one day and then into Houston another. Marty was the chauffeur, driving the Explorer around Texas and Pam was the new Mom shopping expert. She helped Robin to pick out all the latest necessities for the new baby. They made several stops for kid pee breaks and then for Momma pee breaks. They laughed every day. One day they went to the Six Flags amusement park and another day to Sea World. Marty really only wanted to see the Alamo, so they fit that trip in as well.

The meal that Robin had prepared for Thanksgiving was spectacular. To her it was nothing, just a few days in the kitchen. But to her guests it was a delight. The house was decorated in fall colors with turkey and pumpkin decorations throughout the house. Whenever Robin entertained, she put on a show. It was not only for the palate, but all the senses got stimulated as well.

The two weeks went by far too quickly and it was time for their guests to be heading home. Robin and Leesa drove them to the airport and they all said their tearful good-byes. Marty thoroughly enjoyed himself and said he couldn't wait to come back when Lee would be at home and they could hang out together. Leesa was even sad that Jordan was going. She enjoyed having someone close to her own age to play with. She told Robin that on the way home from the airport.

"Robin I liked having Jordan to play with, he was fun."

"Well Honey, after Christmas, we will get you enrolled in a preschool and then you will have other kids to play with."

"I think that will be nice."

Robin and Leesa chatted all the way home. When they had almost arrived Robin said, "Guess what Leesa, in two weeks your Daddy will be home. Two weeks! You sure have waited a long time to see him haven't you?"

"Yes I have. I have been really busy since I came here though. I don't think I would have time for him even if he was here."

Robin laughed, "I guess you're right. We have been busy, but you would have had time and he would have loved every minute of it. Do you know how many days two weeks is?"

"No."

"It's fourteen. That's all. Fourteen. We have to get everything ready for Christmas before Daddy gets home, so we can spend lots of time with him.

The two weeks dragged, even though Robin and Leesa were busy. Robin was so anxious to see Lee and she was getting very excited about all the news she had to share with him. The days were filled with baking cookies, decorating, wrapping gifts and shopping. Everyday they would come home with bags of things they had purchased. Robin had got a couple of the ranch hands to help her set up the decorations in the house and the yard. Pam had laughed at all the 'stuff' Robin had accumulated before she left and now there was even more. Pam had accused Robin of becoming a real American. Robin had laughed saying not only an American, but one from Texas. And in Texas, we do everything big! They had a good laugh about that. The decorations looked magnificent.

Lots and lots of lights hung in the trees. Pine bough garlands strung with clear mini lights and red bows were strung along both sides of the fence that lined the driveway. The large plants in the front garden were strung with clear mini lights also. A large wreath decorated with mini lights and gold bows was hung on the front door. The clear lights that usually lit up the garden were replaced with red and green bulbs. Robin had decided to wait until Lee got home to do the inside of the house. He would probably have preferred that it had all been done for him. But Robin thought that this Christmas was going to be the first of a whole new life for them and Lee would have to be a part of it for Leesa's sake. She could see them all together as a family doing the Christmas decorating and just enjoying the holiday season together. It was going to be a change for all of them this year, a change that was definitely going to be for the better.

It was December the seventh, a beautiful Sunday. The guys would be home tomorrow and Robin was very excited. She had grocery shopped and planned several meals, done the prep work. The house was cleaned and everything done and organized so that they would have time to spend with Lee. Leesa was getting excited too. She had picked out a pretty new dress she wanted to wear when she got to meet her Daddy for the first time. Robin's pregnancy was definitely starting to show. She was wearing maternity clothes and had purchased herself a nice dress for tomorrow as well.

The two girls were outside in the front yard doing last minute finishing touches on the bows and lights, cleaning out the fountain, sweeping the front doorsteps. Robin was wearing a pair of black leggings and a 'Texas Cowboy's' T-shirt, her new tummy very obvious, and her hair pulled into a ponytail. Leesa was in a dirty pair of jeans and an equally dirty T-shirt. She also had her hair pulled into a ponytail. They were laughing and talking when Leesa suddenly said, pointing down the driveway,

"Robin what is that?"

Robin looked up from what she was doing and watched a white stretch limo winding it's way up the driveway.

"It's a limo Leesa. A fancy car that your Daddy and the guys get to drive around in. I wonder what it's doing here today. Maybe they are just checking to see where we live so that they will know where to drop off your Daddy tomorrow."

"My Daddy drives a car like that?" Leesa asked in awe with her eyes in huge circles.

Robin giggled.

"No Sweetie. He doesn't drive it. He is being driven in it. They have a driver, he is called a chauffeur. Your Daddy sits in the back seat."

"Wow! Is he famous and rich or something?" Leesa asked in absolute amazement.

"Yeah-or something!" Robin answered as she came over to Leesa and put her arm around her shoulders.

When the car stopped in front of them and the doors started opening, Robin stood completely still. One by one each of the guys climbed out of the car. They took their turns hugging Robin and patting her on her tummy. It was obvious to her that each of them had known her news. She supposed the wives had told them, and she wondered if Lee knew too. They were each introducing themselves to Leesa and Robin turned to her and said,

"Honey, these are all the guys who play in the band with your Daddy."

"Robin, which one is my Daddy?" She asked with big eyes staring at each of them and not making a connection with any.

"He's not here Honey. Let's go look in the car." She took Leesa's hand and they looked in the car. Leesa was amazed at the size and didn't want to get out. Robin turned and looked at the guys with a questioning look on her face and sheer panic running through her veins. They all pointed and nodded to the end of the driveway. There he was leaning against a tree at the end of the driveway. His arms folded across his chest, his hair long, he was wearing a white T-shirt, black jeans with a black leather belt with the big silver buckle on it and black leather cowboy boots. He looked like a God to Robin. She started walking towards him not letting her eyes leave his for a second. Neither of them ran, slowly they made their separate paths to each other. With arms open they embraced each other with a bond that neither time nor space could ever take away. Lee wrapped his arms around Robin and she around him. They hung on to each other for an eternity, taking in the warmth, smell and familiarity of each other as though they had never been apart. Then he kissed her. A long hunger filled kiss. They were still embraced in each others arms when a little voice asked,

"Robin, is this my Daddy?"

They pulled apart and Lee looked into Robin's eyes searching for an answer. He looked down at Leesa and then back at Robin.

"Lee, I have a couple of things I need to tell you." Robin said with a smile in her voice.

"I can see that." He replied looking down at Leesa and then at Robin's stomach and then back to her eyes.

"This beautiful young lady is your daughter. Her name is Leesa. She has been waiting an awfully long time to meet you."

Lee bent down and shook her hand and then with tears in his eyes, he picked her up in his arms and gave her the biggest hug she had ever had.

He put her back down on the ground and squatted down to her level.

"I didn't think I would ever get a chance to meet you. Hello Leesa."

"You smell good, and you look good too." She carefully observed.

Lee laughed as he put his free arm around Robin's shoulders and said,

"Let's head up to the house. Now I know why the guys all wanted to drop me off first. Seems that you two have a lot of explaining to do."

"So do you. We thought...."

Leesa cut Robin off.

"We got new dresses to wear Robin, how come we don't have them on?"

"That's what I was just about to ask your Daddy. You're not supposed to be home until tomorrow." She said looking back at Lee.

"We decided to take a different flight home so we could get here early. Looks like I should have been here a long time ago though. How long have you been here Leesa?"

Robin answered for her,

"The day after you left."

When they had reached the top of the driveway, the band had already unloaded Lee's things from the car and they each congratulated him on his new family. They shook hands and patted backs and said their good-byes, leaving this new family alone.

"So what's going on?" Lee asked as Leesa ran ahead of them into the house.

"Do you want the full story or the condensed version?"

"Why is Leesa here?"

"Her mother was killed in a car accident, she had no other family."

"Shit!"

"Lee, I had only a few hours to make a decision. Either she came here or would be put up for adoption."

"Are you okay with her here?" He put both of his hands on Robin's shoulders and looked into her eyes. "Honestly?"

"I knew right away that she had to be with us. But I'm mad at you for not acknowledging that she even existed, for not telling me. You have missed five years of her life. She doesn't understand why you've never met her. She was told that you are very busy and had no time for her. Lee you are going to have to pay a lot of attention to her and...."

Leesa then came running back into the kitchen where Robin and Lee had been standing since she left them to go upstairs. She was dressed in the new dress that she had chosen to meet her Daddy in. Robin began to cry looking at this sweet child with her dirty face and messy hair trying to look pretty for her new Daddy.

Lee looked at Robin and saw the tears and he could see the love in her eyes for this child that wasn't hers, but she had taken in for him. His heart broke right on the spot. He picked Leesa up and gave her a twirl around the kitchen and told her she was beautiful. Blinking back tears, he went back to where Robin was standing and asked,

"So what's this?" Pointing to her stomach. With a smile on his face he said, "That wasn't there when I left."

"Oh yes it was. We just couldn't see it yet." Robin replied.

"It's going to be my brother or sister." Leesa said leaning from Lee's arms to touch Robin's belly.

"Can I touch it too?" Lee asked.

"Sure," answered Leesa in a tone like it didn't matter who touched it. She wiggled out of Lee's arms and took his hand and put it on Robin's belly.

"Robin says it kicks her sometimes, but it doesn't hurt her."

They were all laughing.

"Why didn't you tell me about any of this Sweetheart? This is all big news." He thought for a moment. "Is this why you decided to stay home?"

Robin started to laugh. "Nope. All of this was a total surprise. Remember when I told you we hadn't checked the answering machine when we got home from Victoria?"

Lee nodded his head, but he didn't really remember.
"Well….." Robin briefly explained the story to him.

Chapter Thirty-One

That evening after Lee had read Leesa her bedtime story and he tucked his daughter into bed for the first time, he went downstairs to the kitchen and hugged Robin.

"You're an amazing woman Mrs. Cotton!"

"Why do you say that?" She asked, wrapping her arms around his neck.

"I can't believe everything you've done since I've been gone. God I feel like I've missed an entire lifetime with the two of you. Leesa sure does seem happy here and she sure does talk about you a lot. And shit, Robin, you're pregnant! How the hell did that happen? When the hell did that happen? All the years that we kinda tried and we've never really been careful, isn't it weird that it happens at the same time we get Leesa?"

Robin was smiling. "I know, it's like it was meant to be or something. I know this is all so much for you to deal with at once. Here you thought you were coming home to your wife and you find out you've got an entire family that you didn't know about."

"Robin," He took her face in both of his hands. "It's going to take me a while to get adjusted to this. But I will, you know that." He kissed the end of her nose and grabbed her hand and led her to a couch in the family room. They both sat down and he put an arm around her shoulder and pulled her close to him. "I missed you so much this trip. I did a lot of thinking. It's time the band slowed down. I don't want to travel like that anymore and especially now. Look what I missed out on with Leesa. I don't want to do that to this new baby. I want to be involved in every minute with it and with you. You shouldn't have had to do this all on your own."

"I didn't. Your parents helped with the decision and both of our parents helped me with adjusting. Lee she is a wonderful delightful child. You will find out the things I have, there's a whole other world out there. A special one that we never even knew existed and now I can't imagine ever not being a part of it. We were ready for this to happen to us. Look at everything we've gone through and especially me the last few months. It all just seems right."

Lee smiled and pulled his arm back from around Robin's shoulder and he held her hand.

"Is it alright for us to make love? I need you so bad."

Robin took his hand and together they turned out all the lights and locked up the house and headed upstairs. They did make love. But it wasn't like they used to. The passion and hunger were replaced with thought and gentleness. It was far more careful and in fact very awkward. They both laughed a lot and just enjoyed being close and in each others arm's once again.

Epiloge

Christmas came and the house was filled with plenty of new toys. Leesa was a very happy little girl and she and her Daddy bonded just like Robin knew they would.

New Year's Eve arrived and the Cotton's had planned a big party and would officially announce the news to the world. The tabloids had already learned some of the news and as usual were speculating and making up their own stories. Lee and Robin decided to invite the local press early in the day and let them get the story straight from them. The press conference was called for four o'clock in the afternoon of New Year's Eve. There was a very informal announcement stating that Leesa was Lee's daughter who had been born while Lee and Robin had been apart several years ago. Her mother had died and she was now living with them. No more discussion about it. That was all anyone needed to know. Besides people would make up their own stories anyway. The entire band, along with their families were all gathered for the conference and when done with the Cotton story, Rocket Fuel announced that they were taking a year long break from touring and were going to stay at home and work on a new album. After the press had left, more and more friends arrived, and the house was rock'in just like it used to.

Late in March, Leesa was happily enrolled in school, Lee was in the studio working, and Robin was outside puttering in the yard. She got an instant pain. No warning. She stood where she was until it passed. Then she started to go in the house and along came another one. Again she stood still until it passed. When she finally made it inside the house, along came another one. She yelled for Lee. He flew up the stairs and grabbed Robin as she grabbed the counter for support as another piercing pain hit.

"Call my Mom and ask her to get Leesa from school and call your Mom too."

Robin got the words out as another wave of contractions hit her. She tried to walk and keep moving while Lee was on the phone. When he was done, she gave him the number to call the doctor. Then she told him where to find her already packed suitcase in her closet.

He was doing what she was telling him and it was a good thing she was so organized, because he didn't know which direction to go in. He didn't want to leave Robin alone, he could see she was in a great deal of pain, it hurt him to see her like that. He ran upstairs and got the suitcase and then rushed out and got the Explorer. He had to lift Robin into the passenger seat. By now they were both laughing. The half-hour drive to the hospital was the longest ride Robin felt she had ever taken. She was wondering if they would ever arrive.

Almost twenty-four grueling hours later, Lee and Robin were laying together on her hospital bed with their most cherished gift to each other lying between them. Their son. They named him Jackson Brodie Cotton. Robin was stroking his tiny cheek with her finger and she looked over at Lee and said,

"Now our family is complete. Thank-you Lee."

He looked back at her with tears in his eyes, for he had just witnessed the pain and fear that his wife had gone through giving birth to this child.

"No Robin, Thank-you. You have made more than my dreams come true. You have given me a life that I never expected to have, you have given a little girl love and a safe and happy home, and now you've given life to a son for us who will carry on the Cotton name. There is nothing that I will ever be able to do or give you that compares to what you have given to all of us. God Bless you Sweetheart."

The End

I would like to thank all the people who have been so supportive and encouraging during the process of getting this book published. First, my mom who instilled in me the love of books and let me see the world through words.
My dad who is still building more bookshelves, and to my daughter who I hope one-day will see that sometimes a good story can change your life.

I DID IT!!!!

With a lot of help from my friends.

THANK- YOU ALL!

Follow your dreams, who knows where they may take you.

LaVergne, TN USA
13 November 2009
164087LV00004B/105/P